Similar Differences

by
Jay Howard

Foreword

Welcome to my second collection of short stories. Why have I called it *Similar Differences*? Because… well, we're all similar, and we're all different. As they say, we are all unique, just like everyone else. Our base personalities are moulded and refined by our circumstances and the people we meet. Of prime importance are the relationships we form with our parents, our life partners, and our children. In this collection you will meet people assessing their lives and those relationships, making decisions that will affect their own lives and everyone they are close to.

Our reactions to similar situations are not predictable, except within certain limitations, which makes real life interesting and provides endless opportunity for writers of fiction to imagine their own outcomes. If there were inflexible rules about how we behaved towards each other, blindly obeyed by everyone, there would be no more war or hunger, no more envy or inequalities, no 'deadly sins'. Nor would there be any individuality, creativity or demonstrations of human adaptability. It would be a safer life but there would be no music, art or literature, no curiosity or scientific endeavour. That's not a life I fancy living; crazy, quirky, fascinating, absorbing are all good words in my book.

Jay Howard
May 2014

Contents

For Better, For Worse

Sylvia held her parcel to her chest, really tightly, with both forearms and gloved hands. She wasn't sure if she was holding the parcel, or holding herself together. Autopilot had carried her into town, following her original plan of changing the bed linen then posting her manuscript. She hadn't been able to think; the shock was too sudden, too profound. That earring, tucked down into the side fold of the sheet, had tilted her world dangerously, threatening to tip her off into the stygian abyss of the unknown. Going to town was normal, familiar; it would provide the anchor to stop her sliding off the edge.

Not that this particular trip to the post office was entirely normal. It had taken so much work and determination to get to this point. Just an hour ago she had been feeling excited, if apprehensive, believing that Roger wouldn't dismiss a completed novel as 'mere scribblings'. It had taken years to write it, a stolen half hour here, an hour there.

Milly, the editor of a women's magazine she regularly wrote short stories for, had given her the encouragement she needed. "Your writing is so vivid," she'd said. "Sales always go up when our readers see there's another story of yours in the issue. You *have* to find time to finish that novel – I'm hooked already and I've only read the outline."

Without Milly's support Sylvia doubted she would ever have had the courage to contemplate publishing her work. It was meticulously researched and she had been totally absorbed by her characters' emerging story, but was Milly right? Would anyone else really want to read a full length novel of hers? Surely the women who picked up a magazine for a little light reading during a coffee break or while having their hair done wouldn't be interested in taking the time it needed to read a novel... would they?

When she had continued to dither, Milly had used her contacts to set up a meeting with an agent. Before she knew it, Sylvia found herself under contract to complete the manuscript by the end of September.

So here I am, she thought. *But at what cost? Have I neglected him? Should I have made more effort to make myself attractive for him? Why else would he turn to another woman for comfort?* Her mind refused to use the 's' word.

She followed her normal route through the park; when she reached the gates opposite the post office she gave in to the weakness and nausea she felt, sinking onto the bench there, still tightly gripping her parcel. Her whole body felt strange, sensation missing where it should be, noticeable where it shouldn't. Her temples and heart were pounding whilst her face and legs felt anaesthetized. Then the inner quivering started.

Distracted... yes, it's all my fault... What a foolish woman you are, Sylvia Murray! All the things Roger's said about you are true - foolish, unobservant, ridiculously naive for a woman your age!

She made a determined effort to slow her breathing. Foolish she may be but she would not cry in public. The chilly breeze fluffed her naturally curly hair across her face and she tucked it back behind her ears, her movement jagged, irritated. It should have been trimmed quite a while ago but cash had been in short supply since paying her youngest's rent arrears.

Again. I had to; Ginny shouldn't be worried about

eviction, not in her final year, with Finals creeping up. It would have been nice to see her in the summer break...

Her thoughts continued to whirl as randomly as the autumn leaves around her feet.

Thirty years soon... what symbol is it for a thirtieth anniversary? Will Roger remember? Or the children? I bet Ginny won't even think it strange that her father was tempted elsewhere. I've got old and they don't care.

Sylvia felt the burden of all those years, the isolation until the children were old enough for her to return to work, the drudgery of the office job, the endless toil at home with no one noticing the things she had done, only the things she hadn't had time for. And somehow it hadn't got any easier once the children left home. There always seemed to be something that they wanted but had no funds for. Anna's voice ran like a recording in her head: 'I'm not asking for myself, Mum, but I know you don't want your grandchildren to be the odd ones out at school.' *What do they spend two good salaries on for there to be nothing left for the children? And why does it have to be designer stuff these days?*

As for the time she spent helping out still... A text that morning was 'got the wallpaper' – just those three words. That was for her to do the new nursery. *A 'hello' or 'please' would be nice. I tried to teach them manners; are they polite to other people?*

She suddenly realised she'd allowed herself to get sidetracked by the children again. *Is that why he did it? Have I focussed too much on the children? Has he felt left out? But he never pays me any attention either...*

Sylvia wondered just when he'd stopped desiring her. It was just over a year ago he'd persuaded her they would sleep better if they had separate bedrooms, substantially longer since they'd made love. He'd said she disturbed him with her snoring.

Do I snore? Or is that just an excuse, another convenient lie? Perhaps he feels less guilt if it's just his bed he's taking his mistress to, if indeed he feels anything so 'plebeian' as guilt.

Brake off, throttle jammed open, her mind raced over all the small ways he showed he hardly noticed her as a woman.

Convenient lie... I suppose I've always known he lies to me.

She groaned, wishing her brain had stayed numb. The tidal flood of things previously unacknowledged was overwhelming her defences. She was drowning and there was not a soul to throw a life ring.

Perhaps everything I thought was true was really just what I preferred to believe.

Both husband and children were better educated than she had been. Roger was a history professor, her four children were all rising stars in their various careers – *or so they tell me...*

Her once close circle of like-minded friends had evaporated over the years, with her living in a different area after her marriage then staying home looking after her growing family.

He never liked any of my friends – too 'working class' – and he let them know it, too.

Most of all she missed Melanie, with her zest for life, her understanding of what made people tick, her dependable good advice and the way she had of seeing the nub of a matter. They'd grown up together on the council estate and Melanie had always looked out for her gauche friend.

I'm sorry, Melanie, I should have made time for you. I've missed you and could really do with one of your hugs right now, and you telling me, 'OK, so you've messed up again, but we can sort it.' *You wouldn't care that I'm older and fatter and can't afford fashionable clothes. Because I reckon that's what it is - he's ashamed of me. Ashamed, and bored, and knows he's still attractive to women, can no doubt have any one of those bright young things he teaches.*

She knew what Melanie would have answered: 'So you're not a lanky teenager any more, but 'fat'? You're five foot nine so size sixteen is curvy in all the right places, like Marilyn Munroe! Yeah, you've gone up a couple of dress sizes since having four kids. Big deal!'

Sylvia thought Roger had aged much better, though. His Oliver Reed eyes still invited every woman he met into bed, and his cycling, taken up again when the children got bikes, kept his muscles honed.

'I'll take them cycling,' he'd say, 'get them out of your hair while you're busy.'

He never included me in the fun side of having a family. He was forever taking the children out, for their sports, or flying kites they made together, trips to the cinema and pantomimes. *I was always ignored at school plays and sports' days; the other mothers flocked around him,* 'how marvellous to see a father making time for his children', 'I can see where they get their talent and good looks from'...

And homework...

'Don't ask your mother,' he always said, 'she knows diddly-squat about anything.'

And my goodness did he crow about their academic achievement, claimed all the credit, said it was his genes that accounted for their intelligence.

But he'd stopped talking for hours on end about his work when he realised she'd done a great deal of research about his specialist area and had formed her own opinions about what life was like in seventeenth century England, especially for women. Her novel's main character was a young woman from a strict Puritan family who fell in love with one of the Cavaliers who requisitioned her family's manor house. Then the tide of the Civil War changed and the secret lovers were torn apart.

She winced anew at his patronising tone when her novel was first mentioned in public. They'd had a few neighbours round for a meal – w*ell, a few in his book, not mine; he doesn't have to do the shopping and cooking and clean up after ten people* - and she'd finally risen to the bait after Phyllis had been goading her too long, with her feigned concern about Sylvia's 'drab little life' and 'lack of interests'; she'd told them she was writing in earnest.

Of course, it's to be 'Phyllida' now, as it has more 'class'. Phyllida! Doesn't sound classier to me, more like a cream cheese. When did he last say my name, except in anger? It's always 'her' or 'she'...

'So now you know our guilty secret,' he'd said. 'Her fluffy little romance was absorbing enough for her to forget to chill our wine.'

Phyllis had patted his arm and leaned in to him, wafting more clouds of that ghastly perfume around while she filled Roger's glass. 'Never mind, Roger, we prefer red, don't we.' She filled her own glass with red wine too, then pushed the warm bottle of white towards Sylvia.

But it's not just a fluffy romance, whatever he says. My characters and their story are fictional, but it's true to life and they behave in accordance with the mores of the time; all the details are historically accurate. He'd know that if he would only read it.

There'd been laughter down the phone from her agent when she admitted why she sounded a bit down. 'Oh, no,' she said, 'don't ever expect support from the people you know. Family and friends are always last in the queue to take any interest in what you've been writing. It doesn't look like 'serious work' so it can't be, right?'

For the past three months she'd been staying in the office when everyone else had left for the day. It was the only way to guarantee a few hours of uninterrupted peace to concentrate on the final editing. She had a deadline to meet now she was under contract.

'Oh, so it's 'I'm all right, Jack', is it?' he'd said in a mocking falsetto. 'It's 'I've had a lovely meal in the canteen, thank you. I'm sure you can survive on a few scraps from the fridge.''

'You're the one who claims you're easy to cook for: 'fresh, simple food, nothing fancy'.' She knew all too well it was far from simple; she'd had thirty years of trying to come up with something to tempt his palate when he thought gravy was the only acceptable sauce, and certainly wouldn't contemplate anything with spices.

Her book suddenly felt like a curse. She'd been so busy with her writing she hadn't noticed the growing weight of pages had pushed open the lid of the box and let all the evils out into her world. She threw the parcel down. It skidded to the far end of the bench and teetered on the edge. It looked so innocent, but had seemingly cost her her marriage.

OK, so my marriage isn't perfect, but it's worth something, isn't it? I've been happy enough... haven't I?

That earring... Whose is it? A friend? One of his students?

She frequently hosted gatherings at home, but they were Roger's friends really, and his colleagues and favoured students.

'You don't get out often so, just for you, I'll bring the social life to you,' he'd said.

At first she'd looked forward to them, but inevitably got

the all of the work and none of the fun. Roger introduced her as 'the wife' and no one listens to someone not worth a name.

She tried to think back over the women she had met. Which one of them would wear an earring like that? Which one had he shown particular attention to? No one in particular came to mind, but there had been dozens over the years.

No, wait...

There was another candidate for the role of mistress: Phyllis. She'd never liked the Merry Widow. There was something about her that just screamed 'wily' and 'manipulative'.

Well she obviously saw Roger's belly as a lever to get in.

At first he'd left the kitchen in chaos but within a week – *and why did I never query the sudden turnaround?* - it was spotless each night when she arrived home. Which would be about the time she'd noticed that faint, background odour that wasn't her pot pourri or plug-in air fresheners.

No, that was Phyllis' perfume... I recognise it now.

Perfume was well outside her budget and Roger never bought her personal gifts, being more your 'new toaster' kind of man when it came to birthdays, if he remembered at all, but she'd not forget that smell. Phyllis had forcibly sprayed her with it: 'You'll love it,' she'd insisted.

Oh, Roger, all these years and this is what it's come to?

She heard Melanie's voice again. 'Come to, or always been? He was never good enough for you.'

But he's so clever, Melanie, so good looking... I was stunned when he chose me to join him in that lovely old house in the best part of town. He could have had anyone but he chose me.

'Sorry, Sylve, but he knew a sucker when he saw one. I tried to tell you but you wouldn't listen. That fancy house wasn't down to any effort of his; it was his parents'. What he wanted was a replacement for his mother, a new slave. And that's what you've been for way too long. Listen up, girl! It's time you started living. It's not right that he gets the 'for better' and you get the 'for worse'.

On her wedding day Melanie had pleaded with her to stop and think. Her final words before following her up the aisle were, 'Do you love him?'

'Of course,' she'd replied immediately, but even to her own ears, even then, her words had a hollow ring to them.

No, I didn't love him. I was mesmerised by him; I idolised him, couldn't believe my luck that someone so handsome, so charming, had noticed me, had chosen me.

Colour drained from her face as she contemplated the implications of that admission to herself.

All these years... don't ask a question if you don't want to know the answer... never admitting I knew he was straying because I'd have had to do something about it. So is it his fault or mine?

Her phone rang and she answered immediately, just as they'd drummed into her she must, whatever she was doing.

"Mum, hi. I thought you might like to come over tonight and see the twins."

"Tonight, Simon? But they're only three, they'll be in bed."

"But you can still look in on them. You haven't seen them since last Sunday."

She always cooked Sunday roast for everyone, and then it was just assumed she would wash up while they played games and drank wine.

"No, not tonight, Simon, I have some thinking to do."

"Thinking?" Sylvia straightened her spine against the derision in his voice. "Umm, well, you could do that here."

"And could I talk over with you what I'm thinking about?"

"We'll, er, not be here. Another time, perhaps?"

"So you want a babysitter then? Is that what you're saying?"

"Mum, Marianne gets cranky if she doesn't get some 'me time' with the girls on Saturday."

"And where will you be? Why won't you be looking after your children?"

"Mum, are you feeling OK? You don't sound your usual self at all."

"Don't change the subject," she snapped. "Where will you be?"

"With my mates down the pub. It's *Saturday*." There was a pause. "So," he said brightly, "about eight OK?"

"No." She switched the phone right off.

Oh my goodness, I said 'no'!

She pulled her parcel back towards her, patted it and found she was tingling all over, excited at the possibilities ahead of her if she remembered that two-letter word.

It seems the cost of a manuscript is being forced to accept that you're in a loveless marriage; that not only is one's husband a selfish jerk but he's trained his children to follow their father's lead. But I can say NO! Enough!

But exactly how much do I want to say 'no' to? 'Enough' of what, to be precise?

Sylvia leaned back against the bench, recalling what had led her to sit there in the first place.

The earring.

Awareness of her surroundings faded as her thoughts turned inward, deeper and deeper, logically dissecting what had been, what was, and what could be. It felt strange to

18

look into all the dark corners of her mind. The spotlight of honesty with herself found the rusty locks to mental boxes in which lurked truths she'd assiduously sidestepped for too many years. Each one was forced open and the contents assessed.

She was forced back to the present by a small dog sniffing and licking her ankle.

"Heel, Bess!"

She looked up and saw an elderly gentleman approaching slowly, leaning heavily on his walking stick. The dog half-ran, half-bounced to him and wagged its fluffy tail, watching for the thrown treat.

"Sorry about Bess; she has a thing about ankles," he said as they got to her bench. "Are you OK, Miss?" he asked, panting slightly as he sat beside her.

She nodded slowly. "Yes, thank you, I'm fine."

"That's good," he said. "It takes me nearly an hour to get round the park and I don't think you've moved a muscle in all that time. I was worried you'd had a funny turn or something."

Sylvia smiled widely. "No, not a funny turn, but I do think I'm about to start having more fun. There was one thing left in Pandora's box: hope."

He cocked his head, then smiled too, his eyes twinkling. "Never lose hope," he said. "Sometimes it's all we have to keep us going."

Realisation suddenly dawned about what else he'd said. "An hour?" She pulled her coat sleeve back to check her watch. "Sorry," she said, "I'm going to have to dash before the Post Office shuts."

He waved as she ran out of the park and crossed the road with a new spring in her step.

When it was her turn the cashier noted the weight and asked, "Is there anything of value in the parcel?"

"Pardon? Sorry, I was miles away."

"What's in the parcel? What did it cost you?" the cashier clarified patiently.

"The cost? Oh, just my marriage," she replied.

"Pardon?" The cashier waited, pen poised over the registered delivery slip.

Sylvia smiled. "No value at all," she said, calmly accepting her change.

Maman

Conception

The garden gate swings open on a protest of un-oiled hinges. Mme Bourgeois frowns, glares at the innocent metal.

Why did he not see to that when I told him? Pah! Must I do it all myself if it is to be right?

She walks slowly along the ancient paving stones which weave between massed ranks of herbaceous perennials, resplendent in their summer palette.

What should it be? So many options...

Her mind works through her sketch pads, her sculptures, those from decades ago as clear as yesterday's.

A lifetime of work and so little time. Impossible! So much space...

She sinks onto a stone bench, her hooded eyes brooding, her mind churning through possibilities. The Tate's commission for the old power station is challenging. She is excited by the thought of the sheer volume of the Turbine Hall. It will be a space that remains faithful to its industrial past, uncompromising, stark, yet full of light and air. She does not need her sketches now for *I Do, I Undo* and *I Redo*: she can already visualise them in situ, their steel towers and spiral staircases an echo of workmen's feet, the huge mirrors altering perspective and the interaction with viewers, participants in her art.

But the bridge... the bridge needs... quelque chose de monumental... a masterpiece, the acme of all my striving...

She does not hear the drone of bees, or see the play of sunlight on dragonfly wings. Her focus is inward, searching, feeling her solution is only just out of reach, on the edge of her grasp, something she knows but cannot quite fathom.

What will be in proportion? Massif... mais fragile...

A passing fragrance of roses brings her back to consciousness of her garden. A tiny movement near her hand catches her attention. A spider is busy, spinning its nursery web, thick matt grey strands between yellow-flowered cinquefoil twigs that will keep her spiderlings safe.

A breeze caresses Louise's cheek, a kiss. Her eyes light up, she touches her cheek. The years spin away and she is a little girl once more, safe in her mother's protection, her own strong, fearless, clever mother spider, weaving her tapestries, is by her side in the garden and the message is clear. She nods an acknowledgment. Her life's work has all been leading to this time.

Oui, Maman, le moment est venu.

She strides off towards her studio. There is much work to be done.

Her assistant pauses, holding the prepared tray of coffee and croissants, watching the purposeful gait. She knows those eyes will not see her now, that Louise will not want the requested breakfast in the garden. There are months ahead in which all that will matter is the work, the creation, the sculpting of thought into reality.

Incubation

Alice returns to her desk looking thoughtful.

"How did the Q1 review go then?" Beth, her friend and colleague, asks. It is of great interest to her, since she is

22

next on the list to face a quarterly review with their new team leader.

"OK, I guess... But he thinks I'm just coasting, both in work and personally."

"That is so unfair!" Beth waves a hand towards the tower of paper on Alice's desk. "You're brilliant at just calmly coping when some arsehole dumps something like that on your desk. And he has no right to bring your personal life into it."

Alice logs back in to her computer and says, over her shoulder, "I think he's right. I haven't really found anything challenging in any way for... I don't know how long."

Her eyes scan the latest emails. "He wasn't saying I'm not performing well, just that I might benefit if I were to find a stretching objective. You know, career and personal development stuff."

"If he pokes his nose into my personal life he'll be in for a shock!"

Alice can't help but snort in laughter. Beth's personal life is enough to make most people blush.

Her attention is then taken with the latest online news items, one in particular: pictures from the Tate Modern, being visited by one of the minor royals. Alice looks at the picture, her attention not on the person but the sculpture in the background. She feels fear and revulsion shiver along her skin. From what she can see of it, it is the very essence of spider. Memories of close encounters with spiders flash through her mind. She feels the cold sweat on her face and is ashamed that such harmless creatures should do this to her.

Her team leader's words sound loud in her head. "You're a very intelligent, capable member of staff, Alice, and there's no way I want to lose you from my team, but

23

for your own good you need to get out of your rut. Define a goal. Think about what you have avoided as being out of your comfort zone. Set yourself a challenge, either work or personal, to tackle something new, something that needs a bit of grit and determination to accomplish."

She stares at the spider sculpture, fascinated and revolted by it. It is so far out of her comfort zone it almost paralyses her.

So he wants me to be challenged does he? What greater challenge than this?

"Who's that?" Beth asks.

"Not important," Alice says, "this is what's important." She points towards the menacing, looming sculpture behind him, carefully not actually touching the image. "That, my friend, is where I'll be on my day off, on my birthday. There's my stretching objective – curing my phobia by facing it down."

Having dropped the bombshell Alice swivels in her office chair away from the computer screen.

"You're not serious?" Beth, says, her mouth a little 'O' of disbelief. "Are you?"

"You know I don't say things I don't mean," Alice says, her voice calm while her heart is hammering.

"But... you're terrified of spiders... you screamed blue murder when that one dropped from the ceiling onto your arm."

"And your point is?"

"I was *joking* the other day when I said you should go." Beth jabs at the monitor. "Look at it! I *wasn't* joking about the size of the horrible thing. It's enormous!"

Alice smiles. "Yes, that's why it's perfect for the task."

Beth shivers theatrically and grips Alice's shoulder. "Tell you what, if you want the thrill of fear we'll go to Alton Towers or bungee jumping or something."

24

"No, I want the spider." *Oh my god, what am I saying?*

Beth sits down heavily, shaking her head. "I offer you a slap up meal with the girls, and a night dancing, maybe pick up someone *hot*, and you choose a *spider* instead?"

"Entry is free to Tate Modern so just think of all the money I've saved you. You can buy my tube ticket and a birthday ice cream instead."

"Jeez, you're one crazy woman. I'll buy your ice cream when you get back. No *way* am I going anywhere near that monster."

"No problem. I'll go alone." Alice saunters off to the coffee machine, hoping Beth doesn't see how her legs are shaking.

Fruition

Alice had always promised herself a cruise along the Thames. She knows it is a terribly touristy thing to do, something that she'd never admit to her friends that she'd done, but it offered such a different view of her city. It was a promise she had fulfilled that morning.

And much good it did me, she thinks glumly, getting off at Bankside Pier and realising she'd hardly noticed any of the scenes gliding past, had not listened to their guide's commentary.

Her fellow passengers are loud in their pleasure; the sun is hot, sparking glittering shards of light from the river. Her steps are slow. Large in her imagination is the spider, *Maman*, the sculpture that is lurking in the Turbine Hall, just the other side of the Tate's doors.

A hand grips her upper arm.

"Hey, steady there, you OK?"

She nods, mute, her legs weak, barely aware of the burly American holding her upright.

"You look kinda pale," he says. "I thought you were going to faint. Hey, can we have some of that water?" he asks a pavement artist. He accepts a fresh bottle, throws a few coins into the hat. "Thanks, buddy." He offers it to her. "Here, take a sip, it will help."

She drinks deeply and with the back of her hand wipes away the drips running down her chin. "I'm fine now, thanks, it's just the heat."

"I don't know," he says. "I noticed you on the boat. Are you sure you don't need a doctor?"

She stares at the entrance. "I'm fine now." She turns to him, feels small against his size and latent strength. "Thank you, you've been very kind."

"How about we go in together? Keep an eye on you - all part of the rescue package," he says in a joking manner, hoping for her company now that he's been gifted the opportunity to speak to her.

She wants to accept his protection but says, "No - I must do this alone." As she says it she knows it is the truth. And she knows that she can do it.

He looks puzzled. "Huh?"

She looks up at him, her smile dazzling, and sweeps her long glossy hair back over one shoulder. "Your ex-First Lady, Eleanor Roosevelt, once said 'You gain strength, courage and confidence by every experience in which you stop to look fear in the face. You must do the thing you think you cannot do.' I'm about to do it."

He is bemused but shrugs. "It's a strange life, to come all this way and find a very lovely English rose, if I may say so, quoting an American." He releases her arm, finds it hard to release her gaze. "Well, you have a nice day, ma'am." He tips a finger to his brow. "And if you need me, just holler for Leo."

He enters the building. She follows him.

It is cool inside the cavernous space. The entrance has taken her to a gallery. She has no opportunity to hang back in the doorway: there are too many people behind her trying to enter. Wide steps lead down into the hall but she's not ready yet.

There are three installations on the Turbine Hall floor. Peripherally she has an impression of towers, mirrors, spiral stairways, but they are nothing to her: her attention is riveted on the bridge, on *Maman*. Her breath is rapid and shallow. Her skin tingles as fear is swamped by awe. She holds on to the railing, drinking in the sight. The connection is instantaneous and all the more powerful because it was not expected. The chemistry fizzes between them and she knows she will never be the same again.

Steel and marble have been rendered with love and passion into the essence of motherhood. The eight legs, balancing on sharp tippy-toes, raise the ridged body towards Alice, and there, in the ribbed mesh slung below her, are her marble eggs. She is smooth and sharp, fearsome in her protectiveness of her young, all-embracing, inclusive in her oneness with females everywhere. A group of children are running between the legs, playing tag, and they are *Maman's* children too.

Alice feels her awe turn to joy. She hurries down the steps. She, too, wants to touch the legs, to stand within the shelter of the octet of protection, to be, just for a while, a child of *Maman*. She approaches with reverence, walks around and around it, each circuit gradually reeling her closer, the silk thread of recognition urging her, compelling her, towards physical contact.

She does not notice Leo climb the sweeping spiral of a tower's steel stairway, take his bearings as he reaches the platform and sit to watch her for a while. The seat between the mirrors creaks slightly as he settles his bulk. Alice is absorbed in her circuits, her face reflecting her emotions.

She arrives within fingertip reach of a leg. The metal is cool to her touch. She strokes upwards, as high as she can reach. The legs appear to have a fluid form, flowing, yet the joints are knobbly. In places the shaping seems of muscle, almost human limbs, but mostly it is spider, it is art, and life, and wholly unique. Alice hugs the leg, strokes it, grips it tight with both hands to lean back and look up, up, her lustrous hair swinging away from her back. The sculpture towers above her and she can see the uneven spiral of the body, the gleam of the eggs within their mesh. And look – there are nippled bulges, breast-like, ultimate human symbol of nurturing.

The young schoolgirls have joined hands; they are weaving round and through as though the legs are the ribbons of a maypole. The last in the line holds her hand up to Alice as she passes, an invitation to join the thread. Alice laughs and grasps the retreating hand tightly, dances with the excited girls, weaving faster and faster until they go too fast and the line is broken. They stand there, getting their breath back, grinning in delight. Not a single adult has said 'No', 'Be quiet', 'Behave'.

Alice mouths 'thank you' and gives a finger wave to the girls before turning away from *Maman*. She tells herself she wants to see what perspective the tower mirrors give to the exhibition while she gets her breath back. What she needs is to get her emotions in order once more.

At the top of the staircase she hesitates, suspended between the urge to retreat and the urge to accept the invitation in the eyes of the burly man sitting between the mirrors.

"In need of some more rescuing, ma'am?"

Art is Life, Life is Art

The early morning light is gentle, the shadows long and soft. Angling low through the extra depth of atmosphere, the rays tenderly bless the earth, a quiet promise of the day to come.

Alice swings idly, feet up in her two-seater hammock chair. She sees the webs surrounding her, attached between every suitable strut, and wants to touch their delicate perfection, but knows that to do so would destroy that which she admires. She remembers *Maman*, she remembers past fears, and exults in her world of light and peace and spiders.

A perfect orb web has been spun between the vertical A-frame bars. The web shivers in the light breeze, spinning multi-hued colours in its dance with the dawn. A drop of dew is suspended on the lattice. Photons that have travelled ninety three million miles are caught and refracted, creating a scintillating spectrum.

Just for me. All that way, just for me to enjoy a dawn rainbow.

A mosquito flies onto the web, is trapped by the sticky silk. It thrashes in a desperate bid for freedom, every movement entangling it further. Two multi-jointed legs, banded fawn and brown, appear at the edge of the web from within the dark, open-ended tube, sharp tippy-toes feeling the jangling threads. The spider runs down her trap and sinks fangs into her prey. The mosquito's fight for life is lost.

Merci, Maman, Alice thinks, *for everything.* She wonders if she can be the fierce protector, the clever weaver of a safe life for the child growing within her, that Louise Bourgeois saw in her mother.

A shadow falls over her and she turns her head for his

kiss, lifts her hand to take his morning gift of coffee. "I love this garden," she says. "It's where I get all my best ideas."

"Moving to New York wasn't all bad then?" Leo asks and playfully tips her nose with a thick forefinger.

"Paris to New York, London to New York – not so very different."

"Huh?"

"Louise's journey, and mine."

"Ah, yes."

"Today, I think, I am ready to start writing *Web of Life*."

He raises her palm to his lips. "Just make sure you weave me into it, *maman-to-be*."

The Inheritance

Elaine paced the grand entrance hall, impatient for her mother to answer her cell phone. Her heels click-clacked across the tiles, marking the seconds she had to wait.

"Hello?" The voice was sleep-filled, concerned.

"Mom, you need to get here right now."

There was a long pause. "You got there OK then, honey. That's good. But I don't need to be there." Elaine heard a wide yawn. "If you're going to phone me could you at least allow for the eight hour time zone difference?"

"Fuck the time zones!" Elaine bit down on her frustration. "Sorry. OK, then, *I* need you to get here, like yesterday would have been good so I wouldn't be stood here alone today. You could at least have warned me what I was getting into! The solicitor's arranged for the estate staff to assemble here to meet me in *ten minutes* – what am I supposed to tell them?"

Moira laughed softly. Elaine caught the hint of sadness in it and wondered, not for the first time, about the maternal family line's history in England.

"I suppose it would all be rather imposing at first acquaintance, but you'll be fine," Moira assured her daughter. "Just say hi, and carry on doing whatever it was they did while your grandmother was still alive. They know it will take time to sort everything out."

"Mother, I mean it. The time for evasion and half-truths is over. I want answers and I want them *now*. From you. In person. So *please* get your ass on the first plane out of

31

Vancouver this morning." She snapped her phone shut and thrust it into her purse.

Sudden shafts of sunlight flooded through the huge windows and illuminated the wide oak stairs. Half way up, where the stairs parted to left and right, a portrait hanging there was spotlit. The whiskered gentleman portrayed seemed to be frowning, glaring down at her. She responded by sticking her tongue out at him.

"That's not the normal method in these parts of greeting one's ancestors," a man said from behind her. He closed the huge wooden front door as quietly as he'd opened it.

Elaine spun around, startled by the soft, deep voice so close when she had thought herself alone. "And who might you be?" In the male handsome department he rated highly but she didn't at all care for his cool appraisal or the speculation in his eyes. She felt she'd been assessed head to toe and found wanting. She stood a little taller and raised her chin, her expression as cold as his.

"I take it you are the new owner, Ms Elaine Allen?" he said.

"Your tone says you doubt that. Why? Because of my skin? I can assure you the lawyers checked my credentials very thoroughly before handing over the keys and documents." She approached him and attempted to stare him out. "I repeat, *who* are *you*, just wandering into what is now my house without a by-your-leave?"

His whole demeanour mocked her. "On the contrary, I'm following your orders. Believe me, I have far better things to do than stand around here waiting for instructions from someone who knows nothing about the estate, but you're the boss, so here I am. My doubts, Ms Allen, were due to Lydia never mentioning she had a granddaughter." His lip curled sardonically and he flourished a deep bow, Cavalier-style. "David Barker, Estate Manager, at your service, ma'am."

Elaine flushed, not sure how to respond to such ridicule. "You don't look old enough for such a responsible job," she said.

"I can assure you I am," he said, cool disdain evident in voice and posture. "I've been old enough to be Lydia's Estate Manager for nearly twenty years."

Except for the faintest of crows' feet he seemed untouched by the years, at least to Elaine's eyes. He was definitely what is classified as a 'hunk': excellent physique, thick dark hair and amazing grey-green eyes. She'd have put him at about thirty, not late forties, maybe even early fifties.

"You called my grandmother 'Lydia' just now," she said, dragging her mind away from her physical reaction to him.

"That is her name."

She noticed his lips twitch but ploughed on. "Isn't that rather a familiar form of address for one's employer?"

"I don't know the customs in the US of A, Ms Allen, but Lydia didn't think formality appropriate when we were working so closely together, for so long, to keep the estate going. It's not been an easy ride maintaining the value of your inheritance."

"I'm Canadian, not American," she snapped, and would have said more but just then four more people entered the hall from a doorway, half hidden by the staircase, that Elaine assumed led to the kitchen – 'below stairs' as she'd heard the servants' area referred to in British period serials. She approached them, determined to make a better start with the home staff than she had with her Estate Manager.

She held out her hand. "I've just met Mr Barker. You must be Mr and Mrs Stokes."

"That's right, Miss," the old man said, "I'm Basil, and

this is my wife, Roza Maria." They shook hands. Basil turned to the teenage boy who stood at his shoulder. "And this is my assistant, Andrei."

"And this is my assistant, Helen," Roza Maria added, indicating a capable-looking woman of about Elaine's age.

Basil looked worried and Elaine suddenly realised the full implications of her grandmother's legacy. She hadn't just inherited a house and a plot of land. She'd inherited responsibility for the welfare of many people. How many she had yet to find out, but right then she had five people with her who needed to know what their futures held. She made a few snap decisions, keeping her fingers crossed that they would prove to be good ones.

She briefly held Basil's upper arm and smiled at Roza Maria. "Look, I know David and Lydia used first names, and I don't want to be called 'Miss' or 'Ms Allen', so how about we carry on with the first name tradition my grandmother started?" Fleeting smiles gave Elaine the confidence to continue. "Right now, I could murder a coffee. Shall we all go to the kitchen and sit and talk there? If nothing else I'm sure it will be warmer than out here."

Elaine inhaled deeply as they entered a kitchen that looked large and well-equipped enough to cater for an army. "That smells mighty good, Roza Maria."

"I thought I'd better percolate some coffee," Roza Maria said. "I know North Americans prefer coffee to tea."

"You got that right. I'll take mine black, please, in a large mug." Elaine sat at the large wooden table and indicated the others should join her while Roza Maria bustled about serving the drinks. She watched their interactions and saw they were friends as well as colleagues. These people she'd only just met really cared about each other: she was the outsider, the one being assessed.

"OK," she said when they were all settled, "firstly I want to reassure you all that, as far as I'm concerned, nothing much will change for the foreseeable future. I know I have a lot to learn about what the situation is here before I can make any decisions. I'd appreciate it if you agreed to remain here and help me, but I'll understand if you want to move on."

David looked at the faces around the table. Elaine could almost hear the silent conversation before he spoke. "I think I can speak for all of us when I say we've been very happy working here and don't see a need to change... just yet."

Elaine inclined her head, acknowledging the limited endorsement of her presence. She decided it was time to get to know them a little.

"Roza Maria – that's not a common English name, is it? It's very pretty."

Roza Maria's cheeks flushed with pleasure. "I'm named for my Polish great grandmother," she said. "My family came here in the war; my father was in the RAF. Afterwards they settled in Bristol, where I was born, and that's where I met Basil."

"Roza's mother taught her to cook Polish food – you'll enjoy it," Basil said. "My Roza's the best there is."

"I'm sure I shall," Elaine said. "And you, David, is that a Scottish accent I hear?"

"I'm a Derry man," he said sharply. "That's Northern Ireland, not Scotland." Then he noticed the devil dancing in Elaine's eyes. "OK. *Touché.* I reckon we're even now."

Helen told her that she came from the estate itself, but Andrei was Romanian.

"Quite the mini United Nations here, aren't we," Elaine commented.

David finished his coffee and stood up. "Wait until you

meet the rest of the staff," he told her. "Last count I think we had nine different first languages. Luckily they all speak English, to varying degrees, though I'm fairly certain they find another language useful for swearing at me. But right now I must make tracks. I've a meeting at the Estate Office in ten minutes with one of our suppliers."

Elaine watched him head out of the kitchen, appreciating his easy, lithe movements. She could easily imagine him striding out across the estate fields, dealing with livestock or machinery with equal facility. He paused in the doorway and looked back over his shoulder. She saw his gaze linger on the full lips she had inherited from her Jamaican father.

"Umm, get Basil to show you where the estate cars are and come over to the office at five this afternoon. I'll show you around the farm and the village. About half the villagers live in estate-owned property. Oh, and you own the pub, too," he said.

He left before she could reply.

Elaine let it pass that her employee apparently felt free to give what amounted to an order. She needed this man on board if she was to get a handle on the extent of her inheritance. She needed time and she needed support: too many people's livelihoods depended on her keeping a cool head. She turned to her other staff and smiled.

"Thank you for that wonderful coffee, Roza Maria," she said. "I am your devoted slave if you keep providing coffee and croissants to that standard. I am totally refreshed and ready for the full tour, if you have time?"

~~~

The grandfather clock in the hallway echoed its midnight chimes through the old house. Elaine kicked off her shoes and climbed up onto the huge bed that had been her grandparents', and their parents before them, all the way back to 1821; the date was carved on the six foot high mahogany headboard, like it was some ancient monument. She studied the decorative carving, running her fingers over the birds, beasts and plants.

"Everything in this house is old," she thought, "and that includes the staff." Roza Maria was still sprightly, but shouldn't she and Basil have retired years before, she wondered?

She rubbed her tired feet before tucking them under her. It felt like she'd walked a million miles and knew she'd have to get some shoes with lower heels if she were to spend more time in the ancestral pile. The house was huge, a warren of rooms that would take a long time to learn her way around, and as for the grounds, the kitchen garden, the farm, the village… It would definitely take time to get to grips with it all. *Maybe a lifetime* a little voice whispered in her mind.

A lifetime; was she ready for such a change? Did she want such a change? Or should she just sell up and get back to her normal life?

Elaine grabbed her tablet and googled *Arts and Crafts movement*, getting confirmation of her earlier suspicions. The later architectural additions and details like the tiles in the hallway had definitely been influenced by Pugin, and the decorations were very William Morris. As for the contents, the antiques she had seen had to be worth a small fortune by themselves. She was fairly certain she'd discovered a couple of original Pre-Raphaelites in one of the private family rooms, and they were not as grand as the suite of reception rooms and the dining room, with its table that seated twenty people. She imagined the social occasions *her* house must have witnessed.

She leaned forward and spread the photos she had found in a semicircle around her. The one that held her attention was of her grandparents, standing arm in arm outside a church, dressed in their wedding finery. There had been a newspaper article in the box too, giving details of the marriage of Lord and Lady Thatchen at their local church, St Barnabus'. She'd had to check the picture very carefully – *Lord* Thatchen? – but there was no doubt about it being her grandparents. There was another taken from the bottom lawn, looking up at all the wedding guests gathered on the rear terrace, with this huge house she had inherited in the background.

When they'd been walking through the grounds Roza Maria had said to her, "Don't think badly of your grandmother. She was only obeying your grandfather and by the time he died she thought the rift was too deep to heal."

What order had she obeyed? Roza Maria wouldn't say anything else, just that Elaine should ask her mother. She gathered all the photos and settled back into the luxurious soft pillows. She needed to be rested and on top form for the day just beginning, the day her mother would arrive and finally tell her about her maternal family.

~~~

Moira swept into the hallway on a blast of cold wind. "Darling!" she greeted Elaine, with a strong embrace. "I've been too long in Canada; I'm in great need of strong coffee. I'd forgotten just how dire the transport is here. I travel nearly five thousand miles in nine hours and then it takes four hours to travel the last hundred miles."

Elaine hugged her back. "Oh, Mom, I'm so glad you came. I'm just feeling totally lost in a family situation where I don't know the family." Much to her consternation she suddenly burst into tears. "Oh, jeez, what the fuck?"

"I do wish you'd stop this habit of swearing you've got into lately," Moira said. "You've been tense, unsettled, for months, but that's no excuse."

Andrei followed them in unobserved and saw Elaine twist out of her mother's arms and turn away from her, shoulders tense. He quietly took Moira's suitcases up to her room.

"There, there," Moira said, rubbing Elaine's back briskly. "It's OK. It will all make sense soon." She took her daughter's hand and led her towards the kitchen. "Roza Maria, are you there?" she called.

"Moira!" Roza Maria shouted with joy. She rushed forward and pulled Moira into an embrace. "Oh, my dear girl, it is much too long since I've held you."

Elaine stood back, surreptitiously wiping her eyes, wondering about their history together.

Moira took Roza Maria's hand and turned to her daughter. "Elaine," she said, "the first thing you need to know is that Roza Maria and Basil effectively raised me from when I was ten. She was the one who fought to keep me on the straight and narrow, admittedly a losing battle but at least she tried. Her wisdom and love, just knowing that she was there for me, always on my side, made the difference between a bit of wildness and going totally off the rails."

"Oh, you…" Roza Marie's smile creased the skin around her mouth and eyes. She flapped her free hand against Moira's arm, her cheeks flushing in embarrassment.

"No, no, it's true!" Moira took her daughter's hand too. "This is the first piece of the puzzle for you." She looked down at the floor while she gathered her thoughts. She looked up into her daughter's eyes and took a deep breath.

"When my brothers died, my parents, your grandparents, retreated into themselves and I was left to fend for myself. Roza Maria and Basil filled the void for me, became parents to me in every meaningful sense of the word."

"What brothers?" Elaine asked. "Why have I never heard about them before?"

"I'll tell you everything, but please, coffee first."

Roza Maria gave Moira a gentle push. "You two go to the green salon. I'll bring you coffee." She beamed at Moira, held both her shoulders and gave her another kiss, then pushed her again towards the door. "Go! Go! You need to talk."

The green salon was the smallest of the ground floor sitting rooms, designed for a few friends to sit and chat intimately. Moira collapsed into a sofa and pulled Elaine down next to her. "It feels so strange to be back here."

Elaine snorted. "Nowhere near as strange as it feels to find this place I knew nothing about is now mine."

Roza Maria brought in a tray of coffee and iced buns, placing it on the table in front of them. She beamed at Moira and left again.

"Mom," Elaine said when they were alone again, "I've been looking at a stack of photos of people I guess are all family. What happened exactly? Why have I inherited…" she waved her hands, lost for words, indicating the house around them, "when it belonged to your parents? Why didn't you inherit? What happened to your brothers?"

"Whoah, there! Give me a moment, please!" Moira reached for the pot and poured the fragrant brew. "I'll dish all the dirt for you, but let me tell it my way. You can ask questions afterwards." She leaned back with her coffee and her eyes lost focus as her mind travelled back in time. "Why don't you bring down some of those photos," she said eventually, "and we'll talk about them?"

Elaine rushed up to her room and gathered several albums, topping them with a box of loose photos. She sat back down next to her mother and placed them on the table, taking onto her lap the box which, to her mind, held the most intriguing photos, the casual shots rather than the formal occasion photos from the albums. She riffled through them and found the one she wanted. "Are these your brothers?" she asked.

Moira took the photo and sadness almost overwhelmed her. "Yes," she said, and bit her bottom lip. "That's Geoffrey," she said, indicating the boy on the left, "and that's Simon. I took that photo, just before they died." She fished in her purse for a handkerchief. "A couple of months afterwards they went swimming together. We think, from what people on shore saw, that Simon got cramp and Geoffrey tried to save him, but Simon panicked and pulled Geoffrey under with him. They were both strong swimmers, but there's an undertow on that section of coast, where the river flows in, and they both got caught in it."

"So it was just you left?"

"Yes, and, as I'm female, the title of Baron that Queen Victoria conferred on your great great great great grandfather – I think that's the right number of greats – passed to your great uncle when your grandfather died. The family is quite extensive, as you'll find out."

"Is that why there was the rift between you and your parents? You weren't good enough just because you're a woman?"

Moira turned towards her daughter and took both her hands. "No." She looked deep into her beloved daughter's eyes. "It's because of who I fell in love with."

Elaine jumped up, anger blazing through her. "He was a racist, a bigot!"

Moira smiled wryly. "Actually, I think it was mostly

because he was a snob. Your father was working as a street cleaner at the time. You have to remember this was a long time before the Race Relations Act. There was an awful lot of discrimination and that was the only job he could get to support himself while he studied."

"Pops is the finest man I know! How could they judge him just on the color of his skin?"

"That's how it was back then." She looked appraisingly at Elaine. "How it is *now* is that you compare every man you meet to your father and you find them wanting."

"I'm not going to accept second best for a husband."

"No more would I, so we married in a registry office and we went to Canada to build a life together. My father insisted my mother should never contact me or even mention my name to him from that day. But here I am, back where I was born, and my daughter is now chatelaine."

"Grandmother knew about me, enough to name me in her will," Elaine mused.

"She wouldn't disobey your grandfather, refused to take my phone calls, never answered my letters… I got angry and stopped trying long before you were born. But it appears she got round the ban by getting all the news about us from Roza Maria. Roza and I have written to each other ever since I left England." Moira nursed her cup and her eyes lost focus as she stared back across the years. "Everything happens for a reason," she said eventually. She put her cup down and took Elaine's hands. "Perhaps this is the change you've been needing. Perhaps this is the country where you'll find your perfect husband, as I did."

"I don't need a husband, and I don't know if I want a change as huge as this one."

"Whatever," Moira said. "Just don't close off options until you've thought it all through." She went to the sideboard and poured two shots of single malt whisky into cut crystal tumblers. She gave one to Elaine. "For now, here's to my mother, your grandmother, who loved you."

They solemnly clinked glasses, both wondering where Lydia's legacy would lead.

Popping the Cherry

Marie popped her head around the twins' bedroom door. The children both looked up, one face scowling as only a seven-year-old boy can scowl, the other beaming her delight at having got her way about which game they played.

"You two OK there for a little while if I pop down to the greenhouse?" Marie asked.

Heather nodded vigorously, setting her brown curls bouncing on her shoulders. "We're giving Annabel and Trixie their supper," she said, lifting a tiny plastic cup to one doll's mouth, "and then Jody must help me bath them and put them to bed."

"No, no bath time," Marie said, her tone making it clear that this was not going to be open to debate. "No running water or using anything electrical while I'm not in the house." She paused, looked from one pair of grey eyes to the other. "Agreed?"

Heather pouted but nodded. Jody looked relieved. "Don't want to play this stupid girls' game anyway," he mumbled.

"Why don't you put the dolls to bed and then play dressing up?" Marie suggested then left them to it.

Jody went to the window and watched his mother hurry down the path. She was struggling to keep the hood of her rain jacket up, the blustery wind driving the rain almost horizontally at times. He sighed heavily, his hope of getting out to play with his favourite toy guns and bow and arrows

45

as remote as the sunshine they hadn't seen for a week.

"Jody," Heather called, "you're supposed to be putting the children to bed with me."

He turned from the window and plodded over to his sister. He picked Annabel up and tossed her into one of the tiny cots.

"Jody!" Heather shouted. "You've hurt her!"

Jody shrugged and leaned back against the dressing up trunk while Heather settled the dolls under their quilts, murmuring soothing words to stop Annabel crying.

"OK," Heather said eventually, "get off the lid and we'll play dressing up next, like Mummy said."

Jody remained where he was. His moment of inspiration had a devil dancing in his eyes when he spoke. "Not this stuff," he said. "Mummy knew we were playing Mothers and Fathers, so when she said 'dressing up' she must have meant dress up like they do when they go out. Come on!" He dashed off to their parents' bedroom and pulled the wardrobe door open.

Heather stood in the doorway. "Are you sure this is what Mummy meant?"

"Positive," he said, and pulled his father's white dress shirt off the hanger. His tee-shirt was off in the twinkling of an eye and he disappeared inside the shirt. It had been hung with the buttons done up to keep it in shape but his head popped up through the collar without a problem. The sleeves hung down below his knees and he laughed, flapping his arms up and down. "Give me a hand, Heather, roll them up for me."

She sidled into the room and complied, then helped Jody find the ready-made-up bow tie, the one with velcro fastening. She giggled when he started to do a little jigging dance in his finery, especially when he added his father's black leather shoes and clomped around the bedroom.

Jody stood in front of the full-length mirror and admired his appearance. "Come on, Sis," he said, "you need to look smart too if we're going out dancing."

They both looked through the dresses hanging from their mother's rack. Heather found the turquoise dress with masses of sequins on the bodice and down the full skirt. She loved sparkly things. She stripped to her knickers and slipped inside the dress. As it was a calf-length dress for her mother she had to hold it up with both hands. Jody got out the strappy sandals their mother wore with the dress and Heather pushed her feet into the ends, her heels resting half way up the soles. She tried to dance but could only shuffle forwards, dragging the sandals across the carpet. When she got to the dressing table she pulled the dress above her knees so that she could climb onto the stool, letting the sandals fall off her feet.

Jody wandered over to investigate his father's bottles of aftershave. Heather opened her mother's make-up bag, selecting a scarlet lipstick to wipe across her puckered lips. She checked her reflection, turning her head this way and that, smacking her lips together a few times before moving on to the mascara. That turned out to be a trickier job than she'd expected; with the first couple of brushes she managed to get some on her lashes, even more on her cheeks. The third time she poked herself in the eye. Jody laughed at her cries of anguish.

"It's not nice to laugh when someone hurts themselves," she said accusingly. She threw the mascara wand on the dressing table, leaving black smears across the polished surface. She rubbed her eye furiously, smudging the mascara even further down her cheeks.

Jody was now bored again. "What next?"

Heather paused and thought about it. "After you've been out dancing, you say goodbye to the babysitter and then check on the children and then go to bed." She was positive about this as she'd been awake once when their parents had returned.

They both went to their own bedroom. Jody stayed by the door while Heather went and rearranged the quilts over her dolls.

"Sssh!" she said, one finger to her lips. "They're both sleeping well." She led the way back to their parents' bedroom, and let the dress fall down her wiry body. She stepped away from it and went to her mother's side of the bed to retrieve her nightie from under the pillow. "Get your jimjams on," she instructed Jody.

He grumbled but complied. "I can't wear the bottoms," he said. "They're way too long and the waist is too big."

"Just wear the top."

He rolled the sleeves up, and then rolled them some more before he could see his hands out of the ends. "They don't go straight to sleep," he said. "I've heard them making noises for ages after they go to bed."

"I wonder what they do?" Heather said. "I can't see any games in here."

A flash of bright red among the white tissues in the small bin by the bed caught Jody's eye. He reached in and lifted out a limp piece of rubber. "Looks like they play with balloons," he said. "Bet Dad had to throw this one away as he spat in it too much."

They both recalled helping blow up all the balloons for their party the previous week. They'd each had to throw a couple away when their mother objected to how much spit they'd got in the balloons. "It looks horrible," she'd said, "sliding around in there. Yuk! And what if it burst over one of your friends' heads?" They'd both giggled, thinking about it. "It would hang off their nose like a bogey!" Jody had shouted, making Heather laugh louder.

Heather examined the deflated red balloon her brother held up and wrinkled her nose. "Put it back in the bin. Let's find some more new ones."

Jody opened the bedside cabinet drawer and saw half a dozen red balloons there. He looked at them dubiously. "I think these might be very expensive ones," he told his sister. "They're wrapped up separately, not like our party balloons, all in one big bag."

"Pass one over," Heather said. "I'm sure Mummy won't mind if we only take one."

Jody handed one to her and watched her open the foil. She raised it to her nose.

"Smells like my cherry sweets," she said and began to blow it up. She licked her lips. "It tastes like them too - here, you try it."

Jody licked the balloon. "It does; definitely cherry flavour. Do you think Mummy will buy us some fruity balloons if we ask?"

Heather finished blowing the balloon up. "It looks like a cherry, too, all shiny red and it's got a little stalk too!"

Between them they managed to tie a knot in the end. Heather stood up on the bed and started jumping up and down, patting the balloon towards the ceiling. The nightdress slid from her shoulders, freeing her near-naked body to jump higher.

Jody pulled his father's pyjama top off and jumped from the bed to the dressing table stool. "To me, Sis, over here."

She batted it towards him and he jumped from stool to bed to reach it before it dropped back to the floor. Heather took the chance to jump to the stool, Jody jumped to the chair, they both jumped back to the bed, each trying to pat the big cherry-coloured balloon every time they jumped. Their shouts and laughter got louder and louder, their leaps more and more daring, their bounces on the mattress higher and higher.

The door opened. Their mother stood there, mouth open, taking in the scene before her, the scattered clothes, the cosmetic-smeared face of her daughter. But mostly her eyes were transfixed by the red inflated condom. She grabbed up a brooch from the dressing table, captured the condom and pricked it with the brooch pin. The loud bang was followed by a moment's stunned silence.

"You popped my cherry!" Heather wailed, ever-ready tears forming in grey, accusing eyes.

"I... what?" Marie flushed scarlet, and then started laughing.

"What's funny?" Jody asked.

All Marie could do was shake her head, holding her hand over her nose and mouth, wiping away the laughter tears. After a while she got herself together again and cleared her throat loudly. "Come on, you two, you know you're not allowed to bounce on the bed or wear my clothes or use my cosmetics, so off to the bathroom and wash your face, Heather. Jody - put your father's shoes and my sandals away. I'll need to launder his shirt again." She leaned down to pick it up, then hung up her turquoise dress. Lastly she picked up the burst condom and put it in the bin.

~~~

Much later that day, Graeme sighed a deep, contented sigh and dropped a used red condom into the small bin by his bed. He pulled Marie in to his side and she rested her head on his chest, listening to his heartbeat settle back to a normal beat.

"It's been a rather interesting day," he said, "and that was a perfect ending. Thank you."

"You may have noticed I wasn't objecting," she said and reached up to kiss his chin.

"Did you and the kids have a good day?" he asked.

Marie tried and failed to stop a snort. Her lips twitched. "You could say it's been a bit of a red letter day for the twins," she managed to say in a rather strangled voice. She tried and failed to stop the laughter bubbling up again.

Graeme felt her body begin to shake and looked down at her, wondering what was coming. What came were gales of laughter that would not be contained, but he had to wait quite a while before getting an explanation.

Moon River

"'And that's what happens when you don't do as you're told,' the Fat Controller told Thomas, very cross at the bother he'd caused." Meredith turned the page and paused for her son to look at the next picture. She saw his finger move along the words, his lips moving slightly as he read.

Meredith continued reading out loud, wondering how much he'd read correctly. "'Now you'll be stuck in that shed for a week while you're mended,' he continued, 'so let that be a lesson to you.' Look, Chris, see how unhappy Thomas looks?" she said.

She loved how the magic of stories connected generations. As a child she had regularly begged her mother for another of the Reverend Awdry's stories at bedtime. He'd written them for his son, also a Christopher, and now her own son immersed himself in that same fictional world, one that had relevance for the real world.

"Sometimes," she said, "when you're told you shouldn't do something, it may not seem to make any sense, or you don't think it matters if you disobey just once, but adults know what things can cause accidents."

Christopher twisted sideways in bed to look up at his mother. "But I'm not a Tank Engine."

"No, you're not," Meredith said, chucking him under the chin, "which means it's much harder to mend you if you get broken."

She got up off the bed and leaned down to kiss the top of his head, burying her nose in the clean child-smell of his hair. She brushed it down but it refused to stay flat; his hair was as full of energy as he was. Her own waist-long dark hair had swung forward, tickling his face and making him giggle. She tossed it back over her shoulder.

"Time for sleep now."

Christopher snuggled down under the quilt while his mother turned off the reading light, leaving just a small night light glowing.

"Can we go swimming again tomorrow? And make another sandcastle? A bigger one?"

"Bigger? Today's was an enormous motte-and-bailey, complete with ditch and palisade."

"But we could do Windsor Castle next, or the Tower of London," he said, eyes sparkling in the light from the hallway.

"OK, we'll give it a try. But only if you go to sleep *right now*." Meredith paused by the door and blew him a kiss.

He reached up to catch the kiss, grinned and shut his eyes tight. "I'm asleep!"

She pulled the door mostly shut and went downstairs with a light step. Quite deliberately she had brought nothing more than a couple of sketch pads, charcoal and a small box of watercolours. She checked they were in the beach bag at the bottom of the stairs, then stuffed in some freshly laundered towels, ready for the morning.

Just two days in the holiday cottage on the Cornish coast had done wonders to reduce her stress levels. The biggest benefit, though, was creating quality time to spend with her six-year-old son. He hadn't adapted well to school. Meredith had the distinct impression that he was bored. Sometimes a keen intelligence and an enquiring mind could be a disadvantage. She decided to check her options with private schooling that would stretch him more. If they had to move, since she wouldn't contemplate boarding, then so be it. As for the cost, expenditure would need to be prioritised. This holiday might well be their last for a good many years.

She poured herself a glass of wine and went out onto the decking to enjoy the warm evening breeze. The glass nearly slipped from her fingers and her eyes widened when she saw the man seated there, staring out to sea. There was no doubt in her mind. How could she ever mistake that silhouette? Most of her life had been spent following Aiden, getting caught up in his dreams and adventures. Lit from the window behind him, the roughly-cut, leonine mane that skimmed his broad shoulders glowed the same russet as her son's.

She swallowed hard, her throat dry. "Aiden," she said, as coolly as she could, "what a surprise to see you here."

He got up and turned to her. They stood, just looking at each other, so much history and so many unanswered questions between them. "Meredith." His voice was low, throaty. Slowly he raised his arms to her. "I've missed you."

Meredith cleared her throat and resisted the temptation to run into his offered embrace. She'd always forgiven him for everything, all the hurts, small and large, all the trouble he'd got her into through their childhood and teens. He'd been the lynchpin of her life. He had made life fun and worth living.

Yes, she'd forgiven everything... everything except running away. But forgiving or not, she had never managed to stop yearning for him. How can you stop loving the other half of your soul?

She thrust her glass into his hand. "Take this one. I'll get another."

Before she could escape Aiden caught her wrist and

55

turned her back to face him. "Meredith?" He put the glass down on the table and cupped her cheek, ran his thumb across her full lips.

She stood there, trembling, unable to move away, willing herself not to respond. His tawny eyes held her spellbound. Her lips parted slightly.

He released her wrist and cupped her other cheek, raised her face to accept his kiss. As their kiss deepened she couldn't help herself - her arms crept up round his neck, her fingers pushed through his hair.

"Oh, God, I've missed the taste and feel of you, Meredith," he said.

His words brought her back to the moment, the awful fact of his betrayal. She turned away so he wouldn't see how close to tears she suddenly was. She'd cried too many tears; now she had to be strong. "I'll get that wine."

When she returned he was sitting once more, again staring out to sea.

"Beautiful, isn't it?" he said.

Meredith followed his line of sight. The early summer night sky was just deepening through the darker shades of blue to a velvety blackness. A full moon cast a ribbon of light across the gently swelling waves that rustled and murmured up the beach and around the rocky headland of the bay.

"A moon river."

"That was your favourite song," he said. "I'm hoping it still is."

She turned to him, eyebrows raised in silent enquiry.

"'Two drifters, off to see the world'," he quoted, his voice excited. "Meredith, I've seen so many places, so many amazing things, these past years. Will you let me show you? Will you come with me this time?"

Ice water poured over her head could not have turned

her blood colder. "Do you truly not remember why we split up?" she asked. Her lips felt numb and her heart thudded painfully. She felt a howl building inside her, the same howling she had felt when he left her, the howling that only ended when she first held her son.

"Of course I remember!" He took her hand. "Our child can come too."

He grinned, the old infectious grin she remembered so well, but this time she didn't see the situation as humorous. "*Can* come? You think I have an option or desire to go off with you and leave him behind?" She suddenly realised her voice was rising with her level of disbelief and took a calming breath, not wanting to disturb Christopher. "You don't even know the sex of o*ur child,*" she hissed.

She ripped her hand out of his and grabbed her wine, taking a big swallow as she battled to control her anger.

"Meredith, that wasn't what I meant." He groaned, looked at the floor and ran his fingers up through his hair, pulling at it. He looked up at Meredith, covered his mouth with his hands then held his hands out, palms towards her.

Meredith remembered their childhood mime of stuffing wrong, hurtful words back where they'd come from, the open palms a promise they had gone forever, a plea for forgiveness. If she placed her palms on his... She shook her head, retreated a step and held her hands behind her back.

"What makes you think you have the right to come back into my life and try to turn it all upside down? Seven years without any contact whatsoever and you think you can just turn up on my doorstep like this and be welcomed back?"

His face was so expressive, and she knew him so well, that Meredith was able to read all the things he was feeling at that moment. She knew her rejection had hurt him.

"You know me," he said sadly, "foot-in-mouth disease,

all cattle beware." It had been a long-standing joke between them, but neither laughed.

"It's a good job you write better than you speak," she said.

Aiden took a sip of his wine and sighed. "May I start again?" he asked. He paused and his eyes lost focus as he stared out at the river of moonlight. "I really am sorry, Meredith." He glanced up at her but she kept her expression neutral and the dark pools of her eyes gave no clues. "I admit, I was a real shit to you and deserve to be hung, drawn and quartered for being such a coward. My only excuse, and it's a damn poor one, is I was too young."

"I was young too."

"Yes, you were, but you were always wiser than me." He looked at the floor then grinned again, sheepishly this time, looking up at her with his head still bowed. "I do know I have a son, you know," he said softly. "I've even got photos of Christopher."

"How?" Meredith demanded. "Have you been spying on us?"

"Yes and no..." He shrugged. "I've used a private detective a few times. She told me you'd come here on holiday."

Meredith's skin crawled at the thought of being watched, of her and Christopher being photographed without her knowledge.

"I'm not an unemployed wastrel any more; I have the means to support a family," he murmured. "See that yacht there?" he asked, pointing out into the bay.

"How could I miss it? It's enormous." She'd noticed the yacht dropping anchor earlier that day and wondered about the owner, wondered why they would choose this small bay to stop in.

"That's mine. That's what the three of us can go

travelling the world on. Us and the crew, that is. You wouldn't have to pay for a thing, Meredith. Whatever you desire I will buy it for you."

She sat straighter. "So you think you can buy me?" she said. "I pay my own way in life."

Meredith didn't yet command top fees, but she'd seen the prices for her work increasing year on year. She didn't know that Aiden had had a hand in her success. She didn't know who it was who, over the years, had paid whatever it took to own their favourite paintings and sculptures, then anonymously lent them for display in galleries all around the world. She had been unaware of whispered words in the right ears to lubricate the process of her art becoming better known and hence more desirable. But seeing the size of that yacht, and hearing his words, a niggling suspicion was dawning.

"I'm not trying to buy you, Meredith," he said. "I just want you to know that I can take care of us now."

They heard the clang of a bell, the sound carrying clearly across the water on the light breeze.

"That's *Edith Moon's* bell," Aiden said and jumped up. "I named her for you and your song." He gently flicked the end of her nose with a forefinger.

Meredith remembered him doing it when they were young, thinking to tease her. As they'd got older he continued to do it until she demanded he stop. He'd admitted to her then that he often wanted to touch her, but didn't know how to handle those feelings, not at first...

She batted his hand away, annoyed.

He hesitated then grinned and said, "Come on, let's swim out to her!"

Meredith stared at him in amazement. "You don't get it at all, do you? The first thing you learn about being a parent is that there's someone else's life in your care, and that life is more precious than your own. How could you think for one second that it would be OK to swim out there and leave a six-year-old boy alone here? You're not too young now to understand. Your old devil-take-the-hindmost adventures were fun when we were young and there was only ourselves to consider, but that attitude is no good from a father. I guess you're still not ready to be a parent. Goodbye, Aiden."

She turned her back on him and went indoors, ignoring his pleas for her to stay, to hear him out. She locked the door, turned off all the lights and went to bed. It was to prove a restless night for her, though. Sleep evaded her until finally she drifted off just before dawn.

~~~

She woke to bright sunshine streaming into the room and a gentle breeze wafting the net curtains. Her eyes flew wide open as she heard her son outside, in conversation with a man whose voice she knew so well. In a few fluid movements she was out of bed, dressed in shorts and a tee-shirt and down the stairs.

"Christopher," she said, a sharp edge in her voice, "I've told you many times not to talk to strangers."

Christopher squinted up against the sunlight and rubbed the side of his freckled nose. "He's not *really* a stranger, Mum," he said. "His name is Aiden and that's his boat out there." He pointed out into the bay, where the yacht swung gently at anchor. "She's called the *Edith Moon* and you have to call boats *she*, not *it*, because they're as beautiful as the women they're named after. And Aiden writes books which he says I won't like now but I might when I'm older." He dragged his spade through the sand, leaving a deep furrow. "Soooo, if I know all that he's not a stranger any more, is he?" He looked back up at his mother, waiting for her verdict.

"And what about before you knew all this about Aiden?" she said, in the forcedly reasonable tone that warned Christopher he wasn't yet out of the woods. "When you first saw him you saw a stranger, but that doesn't seem to have stopped you from disobeying me."

"But I didn't speak to him, because he was a stranger, so he spoke to me and told me stuff so he wasn't a stranger and I could talk back."

Meredith loved the way Christopher's mind worked, the way he used prior knowledge, logic and extrapolation to make sense of his world, but it could also be very annoying.

Aiden chuckled. "He's very bright, isn't he?"

"Very devious, I'd say - like his father."

Christopher looked from one to the other, looking puzzled, then shrugged. "I've never met my father," he told Aiden. "He went away before I was born to find something."

Aiden looked serious. "What was it he was looking for?" he asked Christopher.

"Mum said he didn't know, and that's why it's taking so long for him to come back. It's very hard to find something when you don't know what you're looking for."

Aiden nodded. "That's true." He looked at Meredith. "But you can be certain the moment he knows what it is he'll be back."

Meredith was becoming more uncomfortable with the direction the conversation was taking. "I think it's time for breakfast." She took a few steps towards the sea and drew a line in the sand with her foot. She squatted and held her son's hands, catching and holding his gaze. "Christopher - you're not to go an inch closer to the sea than this line,

OK?"

Christopher nodded; it was a familiar instruction.

"As it happens," she told him, "I know Aiden from way back. We were next door neighbours for many years." She paused, thinking about those years they'd grown up together, then pulled herself back to the present. "Aiden - come up to the house and help me prepare." She stood and led the way.

Aiden realised she meant more than the meal by 'prepare' and meekly followed. "See you in a minute," he said over his shoulder to Christopher.

Meredith stood in the kitchen, hands resting on the table as she waited for Aiden. "Don't you *dare* tell him who you are," she said as soon as he entered. "He can live with the idea of a new friend who doesn't stay in touch. It would be devastating for him to know he met his father, only to have you just walk out on us again."

"Don't I have any rights as a father?"

"You would if you'd ever *been* a father."

He turned a chair round and sat down, resting his crossed arms on the back. "I'm saying this all backwards again." He paused and rubbed his chin. "Meredith," he said, "I have no intention of walking out on the two of you again, not now, not ever. I'll be forever grateful for whatever degree of access you'll grant me to your lives. I'd like it to be full-time, but I'll accept whatever you can find it in your heart to give me. I intend to earn a father's rights, not demand them."

Meredith put the milk jug down on the table so hard some milk sloshed over the top. She stared at the white puddle as she said, "Just remember one thing, Aiden - it is *my* decision, and mine alone, if and when I tell Christopher who his father is." She looked up, searching his face for his reaction.

Aiden nodded his agreement. "OK. Now, shall I make some toast?"

~~~

Over breakfast the conversation was almost entirely led by Christopher. He seemed fascinated by Aiden and it dawned on Meredith that her son had experienced very little in the way of male company.

"How many books have you written?" Christopher asked around a mouthful of cornflakes.

"Five so far," Aiden said, "every single one written with the swell of ocean waves beneath me."

"On a raft?" Christopher asked. "Like Kon-Tiki? I made a raft with Mum and we tried it on our river back home but it all came apart and we had to swim back to the bank!"

Aiden laughed. "Your knot-tying hasn't improved then," he said to Meredith.

Meredith could swear she saw the cogs in Christopher's brain clicking and rotating as he evaluated that statement. "You've seen the yacht," she said to Christopher. "Why would you write on a raft when you have a lovely boat like that?"

"Because it's more fun?"

Meredith paled. Her son's attitude to life was so like Aiden's: look for the fun, look for the adventure, never accept the easy or mundane.

"You know, Christopher," Aiden said, "I don't think it would make any difference what type of craft I was on, just so long as I could feel the waves."

"And keep your laptop dry." Christopher looked guiltily at his mother. "They don't work very well when they're wet."

Despite herself, Meredith felt her lips twitch as she remembered that particular episode. She could see the funny side it now, but she certainly hadn't at the time, not when his prank included borrowing her laptop to Skype his friend and then promptly spilling cola all over it.

Aiden reached across for more juice and another slice of toast. "I started off working on other people's boats and that's when I found I wrote my best work at sea." He finished slathering on marmalade and licked some off his thumb. "So when I sold lots of copies of my first book I bought a small yacht so I could write my second one. And you know what?"

Christopher shook his head, totally engrossed in everything Aiden had to say.

"I found out it is awfully hard work, crewing a yacht all by yourself. Then they made a film of the first book, and lots of money started rolling in, so I bought the *Edith Moon* and now I have a crew to help me. I can write when I want, crew when I want, and when we call into port I can go and do lots of fun things on land. Perfect!"

"Mum, can we get a boat, huh? You could paint the sea and sunsets and boats and ports, and I'd crew the yacht."

Meredith stood up and started gathering the dirty crockery. "I think you're a tad too young for that yet, Christopher." She put the plates and dishes on the drainer. "Now, it's a lovely day so why don't you go back out while I clear up here? Then we can go swimming together."

"Will you come swimming too, Aiden?"

"You bet!" He paused and looked at Meredith. "If your mother's agreeable, that is."

"Mum?"

"OK, OK. Go on, out with you." Meredith turned and held tightly to the edge of the sink, her shoulders tense. It was all too sudden, all happening too fast. She didn't feel ready for a full day of Aiden's company, which would entail watching every word she said, every minute monitoring what Aiden said.

Aiden held her upper arms and guided her back to a chair. He started running the water to wash the dishes and spoke with his back to her. "I'm not trying to force you into anything," he said, "but please think carefully about what I'm offering. At sea you can paint, I can write, we can both teach Christopher. And think of all the experiences he'll have." He looked over his shoulder at her, a plate in one hand, the dishcloth in the other. "It's an amazing world, Meredith;: let him experience it for himself, not just see pictures in dry text books. When we tie up for shore leave he can meet children and learn how they live, learn their languages, just by playing with them. It will stretch his mind, teach him to appreciate what it really means to be a human being living on this incredible blue planet. It will colour the rest of his life, help him achieve his potential. It will -"

"Stop! Stop! I can't think straight right now." She held her hands over her ears and went out to join Christopher.

~~~

That evening, with Christopher asleep and the balmy air once more tempting them onto the veranda, Meredith felt calmer, less pressured.

"Thank you for a wonderful day," she said, leaning back with a contented sigh. "I appreciate the way you put up with Christopher's barrage of questions with such good humour and, er, the times you turned the conversation."

"I've been the bad guy for seven years," Aiden said, "but I intend doing my damnedest to be the good guy from now on." He leaned across to stroke her arm. "So, will you come with me? Both of you?"

Meredith's mind was whirling with all the possibilities, all the factors to take into account, all the shattered dreams that now seemed possible again. All the hopes that could still be dashed...

"Aiden," she said, looking deeply into his eyes, "once upon a time I thought I knew your soul, but the going got tough and you let me down." She saw how he winced, how much it hurt to hear it, to think of it. She knew about hurt, crippling hurt. "I believe you wouldn't do anything like that again. But I don't *know* that."

"So you're turning me down." Aiden's voice was flat, defeated.

"No, I'm not," she said, "at least, not yet."

Aiden cocked his head in enquiry, in hope.

"Get to know your son. Let him get to know you. Ask me at the end of the summer if we'll come away with you."

He grinned his wonderful, life-loving grin and Meredith had to fight hard not to throw caution to the wind.

"You'll not be able to turn me down after a whole summer's opportunity to persuade you." He winked, and then his expression changed, became thoughtful. He took her hand, lifted her fingers to his lips. "I've found what I was looking for."

A Nice Cup of Tea

Laura parks in front of the sprawling farmhouse and walks back across the yard to close the five-bar gate. The metal spring catch is warm in her hand, the air suffused with the scent of apples ripening on a half dozen sun-dappled trees.

Against her will her eyes are drawn across the valley and the gentle contours of the Chilterns towards Ivinghoe Beacon. She feels her heart start pounding. That's where it had happened, with the Harvest Moon silvering their bodies and the chalk landscape glowing a ghostly white. That memory is all she's had for so long now she finds it hard to remember the wonder, the joy.

"Go on!" The voice in her head is as loud as the voice she heard on that fateful day nearly forty years ago. "Get off this land, you lying whore, and don't ever come back!"

Laura grips the top bar and closes her eyes, raising her face to the soothing early evening rays. She takes a deep, steadying breath, reminding herself that the scene has changed in two important respects: his parents are dead and she is no longer a helpless, naive teenager. But she is still unsure she's done the right thing in coming here. Her feet are refusing to move.

"Whatever you're trying to sell I don't want it, so you might as well leave now." The voice booms across the yard, its owner approaching from around the side of the house.

Laura turns slowly and looks him up and down. "You

sound just like your father, Joe."

The years have not been kind to him. Most of his once luxurious hair has gone and his big frame has accumulated fat. She wrinkles her nose in distaste at his filthy trousers and a plaid shirt that should have been added to the rag pile.

He hesitates, squinting against the sunlight to get a better view of her. "Who are you?" he says, his voice hostile.

With a wry smile she wags a finger and shakes her head. "Tut, tut, Joe. Your mother was a dear, kind soul and she taught you better manners than that. You might have had a happier life if you'd followed her example rather than your father's."

Joe frowns. She can see him trying to reconcile the mature woman before him with his memories of her voice. Many expressions flit across his lined face before the years melt away.

"Laura?"

He steps to her side, turning away from the sun. Laura stands proudly, knowing her appearance passes muster. Tailored light brown trousers and a crisp white blouse are cool and smart. Her jewellery and watch are elegant, subtly expensive. As a confidence boost she'd even gone for a chic new hair style.

"You still look like Katherine Hepburn," he says, a trace of awe in his voice. He reaches forward to touch her arm, as if not quite believing what he sees.

"I hope not - she's long dead."

She notices him trying to suck in his belly. Caught in the act he flushes, tugs on his wide leather belt and shifts his gaze beyond her shoulder. Painful memories hold them both in thrall, immobile, silent.

A blackbird's liquid trill breaks the spell. Laura takes a

step back.

"It used to be the custom in these parts to offer visitors some refreshment after a long journey."

"What do you want, Laura?" His voice is harsh and a small muscle below his left eye jumps repeatedly.

"Well, a cup of tea would be nice."

He scowls at her, opens his mouth to speak, then changes his mind. He turns abruptly, flicking his fingers at her to follow him indoors.

Laura pauses in the kitchen doorway. It takes a moment for her eyes to adjust after the brightness outside. The windows cast a checkerboard of sun and shadow across the room and she can hear the buzz of a bluebottle somewhere nearby.

For three centuries wood smoke has permeated the ancient beams and walls. The aroma takes her back to the last time she stood on that spot. The big wooden slab of a table was where she had done most of her homework with Joe's sister, Jenny, her best friend all through their school years. Echoes of their girlish voices sound down the decades. She looks around, half expecting to see the young Laura and Jenny playing there still.

Her roving gaze halts on the fireplace. Laura feels a strange giddiness and supports herself against the stone door jamb. She remembers the night, sitting with Joe in the inglenook, when he had kissed her for the first time. For months he had gone out of his way to make her feel special. His wooing had the desired effect: she fell in love and yearned for his ever more passionate kisses. While she accepted that it must be kept secret from his father, his mother became their ally.

Laura looks across the kitchen. Yes, even the hob and sink are unchanged. In her mind's eye Laura can still see Joe's mother scuttling between the two. She takes a few deep, controlled breaths to slow her hammering heartbeat. She doesn't want to take a pill, not with Joe there to witness her weakness.

She clears her throat. "You know, I don't recall ever seeing your mother anywhere but here in the kitchen or in the pantry. Did your father ever allow her out?"

"You're still fond of saying bloody stupid things, then," he says and turns his back on her.

"It's a long time since I've said - or done - anything stupid, Joe."

He turns the hot tap on full and pulls dirty crockery out of the sink while the water gets to temperature. The sink is deep and the growing mountain of china and pans on the bench bear witness to how long it has been since he's bothered to wash up.

Laura does not try to speak over the din he is making. She checks there is enough water in the battered kettle and puts it on the hob. She knows exactly where the brown earthenware teapot will be, the cosy, the tea caddy, milk and sugar. Not a cupboard has changed, and everything lives where it always used to.

Joe fishes in a drawer for a tea towel. He wipes two cups and saucers dry and puts them on the table, then sees what Laura is up to.

"Make yourself at home, why don't you?" he says.

Laura just smiles and warms the pot. She opens the caddy and her eyes widen. "Tea bags, Joe? You mother wouldn't like that."

"Well she's not here, is she?" His colour is rising rapidly.

"Nor is Babs," Laura says, "or your boys."

He makes a guttural noise like a wounded animal. "Have you had your spies reporting back to you, then?"

"Your mother told me. It broke her heart when you just

let them go."

"You weren't here," he shouts. He stops, seeming shocked at his own vehemence. He half raises an arm towards her. "You have no idea what it was like," he says.

"I know what it was like for us, but we were so young, we had so few options. It was different for you and your wife. Why didn't you stand up to him, Joe?"

He glares at her, fingernails tight into his palms, his knuckles white.

"Your mother understood about parental responsibility. She loved you and Jenny so much - she stayed here for your sakes. Your father ordered you to stay here for the farm."

He stands in front of her, shaking his head. "Woolcotts have been here since 1705. That's worth something, too."

"And will a son of yours be prepared to take over?" She shrugs, pretending indifference to his pain. "Your mother kept in touch. She thought that one day I might need to know what my daughter's father is up to. You know, the daughter who would have been aborted if her grandfather had had his way, the daughter whose father was too scared to fight her corner."

She gives herself a moment to let the ancient anger subside. Sharp chest pain tells her clearly that her heart will not take more confrontation. She gestures around them, feigning nonchalance. "Anyway, I don't need 'spies'. A woman would just need to look at the dirt in this kitchen to know only a man lives here." She takes a dishcloth between two fingers, gingerly sniffs it and changes her mind about wiping the table.

He grabs it from her, slooshes it through the washing up water and defiantly wipes the table himself. "I'm a farmer, not a housewife." He throws the cloth back into the sink and the water splashes over onto the windowsill.

71

"I wasn't surprised when I heard she'd left you," Laura continues. "It would've taken a saint to live with your father."

She turns back to the hob and pours the boiling water into the pot, pops the lid on, snuggles the cosy over it and carries it to the table. "My grandmother swore that only tea made with water that had percolated through your native soil ever tasted quite right. Mum hated going to an area without our chalky water for the same reason. She used to check the area's geology before deciding where we were going on holiday. Tea just doesn't taste the same in Somerset, she says, but we've got used to it over the years."

Joe slams his hand on the table. "You didn't come here to discuss cups of tea, Laura! Now answer my damn question: what do you want from me?"

Laura puts her elbows on the table and steeples her fingers. "I realise I had a lucky escape, not getting landed with you as a husband." She holds up a hand, palm towards him when he starts to speak. "And you've taken no interest in your daughter - do you even know her name?" She pauses, eyebrows raised. "No, I thought not. Anyway, despite that, she still wants to know about you. She wants you to know you'll be a grandfather next month." She stops and looks across the table. "Could I have a teaspoon? The tea needs a stir."

Joe turns back to the sink and suddenly thrusts his face towards the window. "It's that bugger back again!" He dashes to the wall rack, grabs his rifle, then stealthily opens the back door.

Laura goes to the window and sees a stag down at the edge of the wood. As Joe raises the gun to his shoulder she barges against him, sending him reeling. As he falls the gun goes off and the stag leaps away, back into cover.

"You stupid cow! That's how accidents happen." He

gets to his knees and jabs a finger towards the wood. "I've been after that one for weeks. I'd have had him this time, but no, you come swanning back and find another way to screw up my life!"

Laura raises her chin, her eyes disdainful as she watches him clamber back to his feet. "I'm telling you about your grandchild but a stag is more important to you?" She turns on her heel.

He watches her walk away then goes to replace the gun in the rack. His work-roughened fingers caress the stock.

Laura sits back at the table, cradling her temples with both hands. She looks at him sadly. "Your father turned you into a clone of himself. Why did you let him do that, Joe?"

Joe stands hunched over in front of the gun rack while the wall clock loudly ticks off the relentless, painful seconds.

"Daisy," he says. "Her name's Daisy."

The words sound wrenched from him. He hides a sniff in a loud harrumph and fishes around in the drawer underneath the rack. He returns to the table and sits down heavily, shoulders slumped.

"They were always your favourite flowers; open, guileless you said."

"And strong," Laura added. "It doesn't matter how many times they're chopped back, they carry on and flower again."

"Daisy... she's a bit old to be starting a family, isn't she?" he says.

Laura doesn't tell him why Daisy needed to be as resilient as the flower she was named for; her anguish each time she miscarried is still too painful, too personal.

He watches her for a while then pushes a pad and pen towards her. "Put her address and married name down there," he says gruffly. "I'll think about it."

"You'll *think about it*?" She crosses her arms and sits back in her chair, studying him with narrowed eyes.

He squirms sideways, making the beech stretchers creak within the chair legs. "You are going to tell me, aren't you?"

"All these years you've made no effort to contact me, no effort to get to know your daughter. Can you give me one good reason why I should let you into our lives now?"

"Because that's why you came here? Isn't that what she wants?"

Laura sits forward and stares at him for a long time.

"I've kept my promise to Daisy," she says eventually. "Now then, shall I be mother?"

She reaches for the teapot and holds it aloft, letting the questions hang between them in the dust mote laden air.

The Scent of Autumn

The blue haze rising lazily into the still air was now close enough for the evocation of autumn to tantalize her nostrils. Adele had first seen it across the fields, the last bend revealing the village nestling among the farms she knew so well. She had slowed to take in the view before dropping down the hill to the church, mentally shifting gears back to her home environment after such a long absence. She had watched one of her neighbours making the most of the fine weather; his plough's last careful circuits of the day, followed by crows and seagulls searching the rich brown loam furrows for worms and insects, was hypnotic, soothing. Her shoulders had relaxed as the tension and strain of her long journey melted away. The flutey calling of a mistle thrush accompanied the lowing of cows as she parked up; the sounds of home.

The verger was busy at the far end of the churchyard, stoking a brazier with trimmed-back branches and leaves raked from between the headstones. Late season apples in the orchard across the road added their ripe fragrance and the relaxed trilling of a blackbird completed the sensory cycle; she was transported back to her childhood, back to just such an evening twenty years ago. She sat there, eyes closed, feeling the day's end warmth of sunbeams laid low across the ancient scene, the golden light illuminating both the present and her recollections of a day that had proved so important in decisions made both then and much later. She was not yet thirty, but so much had happened in her life; had she really once been that little girl with her grandfather?

~~~

"Can I have a go, Grampa?" Adele asked her grandfather.

He smiled at the thought of her using the spring rake; it was taller than she was, but he handed it over for her to try. She took it, looking very serious and determined to do it right, but started off by trying to push it. He reached round her, placed his hands over hers, and demonstrated how to pull the leaves into a pile. "Just walk backwards, little light strokes across the grass," he said. "That's the way, well done. We'll soon have this lot cleared up, eh?"

She grinned up at him. He could see she was relieved he was helping her; she was an independent soul and would never ask for help or admit defeat, even though the rake was much heavier than it looked. The tip of her tongue crept out of the corner of her mouth as she returned her attention to the ground, concentrating hard on the task. The rake bounced unevenly over some uneven ground, individual fingers moving to their own rhythm. "Look, Grampa!" she said. "It's like it's playing my piano."

"With that many fingers it could play a duet all by itself." He made the rake bounce even more and was rewarded with a giggle. She hadn't done much of that for the last year, not since her parents died in the car crash.

"I like it best when Nan plays with me," Adele said. "Much better than when she makes me practice scales."

"But it's only through practising the things we don't like, that we get to do things we do like really well," he said. He dropped the rake on the ground and stooped to pick up a big armful of leaves to put in the wheelbarrow.

76

From the corner of his eye he saw her reach her small arms as far around the leaf pile as she could, trying to match the size of his own load. The wheelbarrow was soon full and together they wheeled it over to the old brazier.

"Remember how thrilled we all were when you passed your Grade III?" he asked Adele. She nodded and beamed a toothy smile. "Well, you couldn't have done that without your scales and arpeggios. But passing exams, that's not the point of them. They're exercises that strengthen your fingers, make them more agile on the keys. And the more you practice, the more your fingers can fly across the keys without you even having to think about it. Only then will the music you enjoy so much sing out with the voice it's meant to have."

"What did you have to practise, Grampa?"

He thought about it a while, leaning on the rake. "You know I love my gardening..." Adele nodded solemnly. "Well there's one job I never have liked, so at first I didn't do it very well: cleaning and sharpening my garden tools. But I found that I couldn't dig a good deep bed if I started off with a fork that had hard, dried-on soil from the last time I used it, and I couldn't get a good clean cut on a stem if the secateurs were blunt. My plants couldn't thrive if I didn't practise taking better care of my tools. It was a bit like your scales; I didn't want to do it but what I did want to do wouldn't be as good if I didn't."

He dumped more leaves in the brazier and stood back for Adele to add hers. "Nothing worth having comes easily."

"Nothing at all?" Adele squinted up at the sun. "I don't have to practise anything to enjoy sunshine. Sunshine's worth having."

"Very true," he said. "We mustn't ever forget how to enjoy the beautiful things around us, my little chick." He

77

gently pinched her nose between index and middle fingers, pretended with his thumb between them to have pulled off her nose. She completed the ritual by pulling his thumb to pop it back on her face.

He raised his face to the evening light, used that as an excuse to take a breather before going back for another pile of leaves. "Old Mother Nature, now, she's been practising what she does for a long time, and she does it rather well, don't you think?"

Adele nodded again and watched him get out his matches to light the bonfire. The dry leaves and twigs caught quickly, blue tendrils of smoke twisting up through the branches of an ancient apple tree that he'd tended all his married life. Together they watched the smoke rise into the clear blue that was just starting to shade towards night in the east.

"How does nature practise, Grampa?"

"That's a very good question, Adele, one that philosophers and scientists have been asking for thousands of years. It was Charles Darwin, though, who first pulled all the ideas together, along with his own observations and conclusions. He published his book, *The Origin of Species*, so that everyone could read it and think about it, debate what he said to see if they agreed." He paused to pull a stray leaf out of Adele's hair. "Put very crudely, nature's way is survival of the fittest, meaning the ones best suited to survive in their environment. He saw evidence Mother Nature often doesn't get it right first time, and if something she's made doesn't work, well its kind just dies out and another species has a chance instead."

He could see one thought after another chase the expressions across his granddaughter's face.

"So what did Charles..."

"Darwin."

"... Charles Darwin have to practise?" she asked.

"He had to practise lots of things: how to observe carefully, how to record what he saw and think about what he saw, how to gather evidence to prove or disprove his theories about what he saw. But first he had to practice how to walk on a rolling ship without falling over," he mimed reeling about as though on a moving deck, "or wanting to throw up overboard." He mimed that too and was thrilled to get another chuckle; two in one day was rather a large mark of progress. "The poor man suffered terribly with seasickness. We're talking about the old days now, with William IV on the throne and Victoria still a young girl; days when sailing ships like the Beagle, the ship he sailed round the world on, didn't have fancy stabilisers like ships do now." He held his many-pocketed sleeveless jacket out to each side. "Come on, Adele, hold your sails out to the wind! Let's skim across the ocean wide."

They both weaved between the trees, rolling side to side as from a high wind.

"Drop anchor, me hearty, we've a cargo to pick up here," he called, stopping at another leaf pile.

"Where did he go, Grampa? Where did Charles Darwin sail to?"

"Lots of places: all round South America, on to Australia, round the tip of Africa, but where people most remember now is The Galapagos Islands, just off Ecuador, in the Pacific. I'll show you on a map when we get in."

They each took more leaves and twigs to the brazier and he supervised Adele while she fed the old iron drum. Orange flames licked up hungrily, consuming the orchard waste with crackling voracity.

"What did he see in those islands, Grampa? Were there monsters? Is that why people remember him going there?"

"Wherever Darwin went he saw evidence of the plants

79

and creatures that had died out, leaving behind their bones and what-have-you as fossils. He realised you could tell how old the fossils were by the rocks they were buried in, and you could also tell what kind of environment they'd lived and died in. Nature didn't give up when she made mistakes, though, and a good job too or we wouldn't be here now.

"Darwin saw living creatures that showed how nature had tried out little differences; differences that made them better able to live where they were. Each of the Galapagos Islands is slightly different from the others, and he saw that each island had finches that were slightly different to the finches on the other islands; the little changes made them better suited, not for other islands but for their own particular island conditions.

"For thousands of years people have practised nudging Mother Nature in the direction we want it to go, in getting the right differences for our needs; think of all the breeds of sheep and cows and dogs, just for starters. This tree here," he patted the gnarled trunk, "is the result of them working with what nature gave us - crab apples - to make what we were given that little bit better. Now Nan can pick Bramleys to make your pies."

He paused to let that, too, sink in, to allow the whirling cogs of her mind assimilate it all. He felt so proud of her keen intelligence, so like his son's. He was ready for another question but was surprised by what the next question was.

"Why are they always 'she'?"

"Pardon?" he said. "Why is what always 'she'?"

"Ships are 'she', nature is 'she', cars and trains are 'she'... I heard you, yesterday, talking to Tim's dad about his new car. 'Isn't she a beaut,' you said."

He nodded and poked the brazier contents about with a

long metal rod. "That's the nub of the matter," he said. "If it's beautiful it's female."

Adele snorted. "Cars aren't beautiful!"

"They are to men, and it's mostly men who control language, just like it's men who are the ones who write history. But that's a whole other story in itself. Come on, we're slacking. Those potatoes we put in the bottom to bake for our tea won't be very nice if we let the fire go out."

~~~

Her grandparents had filled the void her parents left, filled it with love, understanding and sound advice that had set her feet firmly on her life's course. 'There's one person you can't ever run away from,' Grampa had told her once, 'one person who won't ever leave you: yourself. Be honest with yourself, learn what you want and need from life and go balls out to get it. You mustn't ever expect someone else to make you happy; you have to do that for yourself.' She smiled, remembering how she'd thought he'd said something naughty and challenged him on it; he'd spent the next hour teaching her about Watt and his steam engines with their centrifugal governors.

"Hello, Adele." The deep voice was soft, full of love. "Come to see the family?"

She opened her eyes and gazed steadily at the man whose voice she knew as well as her Steinway's. She was surprised to see the first faint beginnings of grey at his temples, for he was not that much older than she was, but he was still in very good shape. Her absence of just over a year for this latest tour was allowing her to see changes she might not otherwise have noticed.

"Hello, Tim," she said. "Your duties for the church are

still keeping you fit I see."

"Amongst other things," he said.

Adele smiled, knowing how hyperactive he had always been, energy always put to good use on the family farm and helping neighbours. Tim opened the door for her and she got out of her car, gathering from the passenger seat the fresh flowers she had brought for the graves she was visiting. They walked together to the family plot, a secluded corner near a yew tree that had seen many generations laid to rest.

"You've kept it nice for them," she said. "Thank you." She traced her fingers over the black lettering on the white marble. Her parents, her paternal grandparents, all here together in two graves, side by side. Other family members were nearby, in company with generations of villagers who had all worshipped in the fifteenth century church. The headstones gave hints of the story of all their lives, hints that gained flesh from perusal of the archives and a little imagination.

She felt Tim watching her and knew he read her thoughts; he'd always been able to do that. He took the vases from the graves and went to the tap by the wall to get her fresh water, then waited silently while she arranged the flowers. Together they stood, remembering times past. Her hand stole into his and tears shimmered in her eyes but did not fall. He lifted her palm to his lips.

"I wish you'd spend more time here with us," he said and kissed her fingertips. "More time with me."

She sighed and leaned her head against his shoulder. She felt his gentle kiss on her chestnut curls, like a benediction, and he moved his arm around her to draw her in closer.

"You're a home-bird, Tim," she said into the warm softness of his lumberjack shirt, "whereas I have itchy teet." She leaned back to look into his clear grey eyes. "Grampa walked me across the globe every night. We talked of all the places he'd like to have seen, the people who went there and the things they did. I want to actually see them all, not get to his age and have regrets about missed chances. But more important than that, there's so much more I have to discover in my music; it's only when I play in a concert, when I feel all those people living the notes with me, that it all finally makes sense." She pushed away from him, turned back to the grave. "I'm sorry, but I'm not ready to give that up yet."

"I'm not asking you to, Adele," he said. He stood behind her, held her upper arms. "Do you love me at all?" he whispered.

"You know I've loved you since you first dipped my pigtails into your pot of poster paint." They both laughed at the memory. "That was the first time since the funeral I'd thought of anything or anyone else. You were the one who first brought me back into this world."

"Then if you love me, marry me. Go on your concert tours, but come home to me. I'd rather have some of your time than just chance encounters in a churchyard. Let me be the one you phone from faraway places, the one you tell of your adventures, your triumphs in the concert halls. And one day, when you're ready, you'll find that living in one small village, really getting to know the people around you, you'll see all the facets of what makes us human, right here in this one small community. The rest is just scenery. All the passions, emotions, the varying degrees of intellect, the concern for each other; it all happens right here on my own doorstep. Please, Adele, let it be *our* doorstep." He kissed her, softly; she felt all his love flow in the gentle touching of lips. "There'll never be anyone else for me, only you." His voice had gone husky and he cleared his throat, clearly feeling self-conscious, his soul exposed.

"I think I've been away from home too long this time," she said. "I didn't realise until today how much I've missed England." She moved back against him, felt his strength enfold her. She twisted round to look at his well-known features, every line and curve that she'd seen change from boy to man. "I've missed you."

"Is that a yes, then?"

"Hold on, I didn't say that." She felt panic set in and took a step back, holding her hands up defensively.

"At least tell me you'll think about it."

An impish grin spread across her face. "Feed me and I'll give you a 'maybe'."

He laughed and took her hand, leading her back through the lengthening shadows. "I'll never understand how someone who loves her food so much can stay as slim." He lifted the rake he'd left by the brazier and tamped down the flickering embers. Sparks fluttered up around them, dying as they watched.

"I love the smell of bonfires," she said.

"We'll both smell of bonfires now." He rummaged amongst the ashes then hooked out two shapes wrapped round with fire-blackened foil. "How about some bonfire food? Jacket potatoes do for a meal?"

"They could be the start of something good."

They left the churchyard under the unblinking gaze of a barn owl.

Tomorrow is Another Life

"I know a very good clinic," he said, "very discreet. I'll make the appointment for this week."

Daphne lay there, stunned, doubting for a moment that she'd heard him correctly.

"Tell your manager we're going away for a long weekend."

"A... a long weekend?"

"You can get rid of it and go back to work on Monday with no one the wiser."

And then he just rolled over; turned his back to her and was asleep in minutes.

She sat up and pulled her pillow from behind her, held it tight to her chest and rocked herself as the wail of despair built up inside. She bit down hard on her lip, pulled her knees up to her chin and buried her head in the pillow's downy softness. The despair ebbed as she rocked and rocked, arms tight round her legs. It wasn't a passive dissipation; it was swamped under the primal force of a tsunami.

'It'! My baby's not an inconvenient thing *to be disposed of. He intends to kill my child. He expects me to lie there and passively accept their scraping, murderous invasion of my womb.*

Rage blossomed into a bloom of fire and passion, crimson and black behind her eyelids.

Her face was an impassive mask when she looked at her husband. Her legs slid slowly back down the bed and she

85

clenched the sides of her pillow, twisted sideways to hold it above his head. *A minute*, she thought, *just one short minute, to make him pay for his treachery.* But her hands halted with the pillow a few inches from his face; even pushed to the limit of her control she couldn't do it, held back by the last vestige of reason that fought its way to the surface.

No, there has to be another way, a wiser way. Make him suffer; yes, he should pay for his sins. And I must keep my child safe.

She had no doubt he was serious. So far she'd allowed him to dictate the rules governing their lives. *All I ever wanted in exchange was children. He knows that. And now the self-centred bastard thinks he has the right to deny me even that.*

Daphne was accustomed to hiding her innermost feelings from the world; her father had thought her beautiful, said she deserved better than the husband she chose. *Choice of husband – bah! What choice?* She'd never attracted male attention. Her hair was admired, or rather envied, by women; it had always been thick and lustrous, with a natural wave and the colour of burnished conkers. Her body, though... her father called it 'willowy'; the girls at school, no doubt the boys too, described her as short and skinny, amongst other derogatory comments. Attracting the attention of a young man as handsome as Ron had overwhelmed her normal good sense, but she'd accepted her less than ideal situation once she was married. No one else would be likely to want her as a wife and she yearned for children.

She lay back down, used her much-practised breathing exercises to slow her heart rate and clear her mind. The night's seconds ticked away while she stared at the ceiling. She was a woman who considered all the options before making major decisions, and now she must act in her child's best interests. For several years she had acted covertly to protect herself, 'just in case' insurance. Now he had proved she had been right not to trust him it was time to play her trump card.

And so the plan was born.

~~~

It was a beautiful bright morning, a most auspicious start to her new life. Daphne closed the front door, the last time she would ever do so. She hadn't felt so light of heart since her wedding day, and drew in deep lungfuls of crisp, narcissi-scented air with a big smile. She touched her face lightly, suddenly realising how unused to the feel of smiling she'd become. Soon someone very special would smile back at her; they would share smiles and laughter and all the good things life had to offer that she would provide.

Sale of the house had been easy. She'd certainly had enough practice. Her father had bought her the first house, insisting only her name went on the deeds. After that Ron had found it was easier for him to have it that way. All he had to do was say, "We're moving the month after next to xyz," and leave her to cope with it all: the estate agents, the solicitors, the packing, removal and utilities. Yes, she had it all down to a fine art, knew all the tricks to make it happen fast and smoothly.

She waved as the small removal lorry rolled off the driveway, taking her personal treasures to a storage facility several hundred miles to the north. Her plan had called for a clean break, but there were things her parents had left her, things she felt a great attachment to, that belonged in her new home when she was ready for them. *I'll just have to be careful how and when I retrieve them.*

For the first time she saw their frequent moves in pursuit of Ron's career as an advantage; it meant she knew intimately many towns and cities in which to lay false trails, a web of deception to prevent, or at least hinder, him ever finding her again. Daphne had no doubt he would try to track her down, at least in the early days, to force her to give up her evidence, but he'd always underestimated her. He would be hampered in the search by his own certainty that he was cleverer than she was, and by the demands of his oh-so-important career. He might not even believe she had the documents which would destroy his reputation, or choose to think that she would never release them. He saw her as meek, pliant to his will, and she would have remained so if...

She took a deep breath and squared her shoulders, pulled her mind back to the task in hand. It was time to use her formidable organisational skills on her own behalf.

The Man with a Van she'd hired had been most helpful, following without comment her instructions about what was to go in bin bags, destined for the tip. He'd stuffed them in the van around the electrical goods without even what her mother would have called 'a queer look'. No doubt he'd seen similar situations before and might well decide to sell them on, but such a possibility, or even probability, was of no concern to her. Another van owned by the Red Cross charity shop in town had taken other things she didn't want or need.

She paused to listen to the birds competing with each other in their early spring mating calls but decided against refilling the feeders in the back garden. She had several tasks to complete before heading off to the first of her meticulously planned destinations. Besides, the new owners would be arriving soon; there was seed in the shed if they chose to feed her saucy, squabbling sparrows. The hedges were alive with them and she mentally bid them a fond farewell as she climbed into her car.

First she delivered the keys to the solicitor and signed the final paperwork for the house sale. She went for a leisurely swim while she waited for the funds to clear then went to the bank; she wanted an overt card trail, knowing Ron would use his masonic contacts to try and uncover her whereabouts, plus plenty of cash for the covert side of her plan. She wanted him to know she was in five different cities, seemingly simultaneously, but have no warning about how or when she was moving from one to the other; rail and bus tickets would be cash purchases, as would her final move when Daphne Richards would disappear off the face of the earth and Marie-Anne Mesurier would take up residence in France.

It's going to be a tiring week, little one, she thought as she pushed open the glass doors and entered the bank's foyer, *but then we can relax together before your birth, safe in the sunshine of our other country. As you grow up you will absorb French chic with the air that you breathe. Your very accent will have men falling at your feet, desperate to please you. But being French you will have the savoir-faire to use them, to pick and choose, to say 'no' until you find the right one.*

She was certain it was a daughter she carried. She didn't know why she felt so certain, and sometimes wondered if it was just wishful thinking, but from the start it had felt right to 'talk' to her little girl.

At the bank she was ushered through to the safety deposit box room and left there in privacy. She filled the travelling case she carried with the contents of her box, all the copies of documents she had made before Ron shredded them, carefully hoarded against just such a rainy day. Then she transferred the majority of her funds to a Swiss account she had opened ready to receive what for many people amounted to a small fortune. She was not rich by any means, but certainly the house sale and her investments had amounted to sufficient for her to raise her daughter comfortably, to pay for her to go to university and start her own life.

Ron was always meticulously polite, charming even, to people who could help him, but had mentally dismissed his wife as a nonentity, hardly noticing if she was present or not. When serving refreshments in the study or taking notes for Ron she'd paid careful attention to his conversations with his many business visitors, and those on the phone. She'd played the stock market accordingly and done rather well at it with so much insider information. Ron had no idea she kept an account separate to the joint one, had no idea she no longer needed her job to pay the bills, but she was certain his contacts would soon unearth its existence, so she left just enough in it to make him think she was still in England with a little nest egg kept secret from him.

Last stop in this town, ma petite fleur, then we'll be on our way.

Daphne handed an envelope to the woman on the motorcycle couriers' reception desk. "Please ensure it is delivered no earlier than 3pm, no later than 4," she said. That would ensure he was still in the office, but too late to do much until the morning.

~~~

Zara checked her makeup in the compact mirror and reapplied delicate pink lip gloss. A quick spray of *Kiss* and she felt ready. Already she had hints he was slipping out of her grasp and needed every trick she knew to keep him interested. At the very least she wanted her six month contract renewed. She stood and smoothed down her navy pencil skirt, the one with the discreet slit up the back that she knew Ron found sexy. He had a thing about the backs of her knees, liked to lick and nibble them when they made love, and knew he always watched her walk away from him when she returned to her desk.

She knocked and went straight in. "This has just been delivered by courier," she said. "It's marked for immediate attention."

She was aware of his focus on the shine like wetness on her full lips as she spoke, was pleased she could still divert his mind from work to her body.

"Thank you, Zara," he said, accepting the envelope. "I'll deal with this and then I think we'll call it a day."

Satisfied with the promises she saw in his eyes for what would follow, she smiled and sashayed back to her own desk.

Ron waited, the envelope disregarded, until the door was shut. He longed to get her alone, to taste those luscious lips, to drown in the smell of her, and feel her voluptuous body tight against his once more. When she became his PA he'd not been able to get enough of her soft, full curves, but after five months the urge was less frequent. It was the same every time he got a new one, which was quite frequent. The inconvenient loss of continuity in work flow was well worth the variety afforded; he enjoyed the chase almost more than the conquest, and it meant none of them got to know too much. He trusted no one but himself.

He turned the envelope over, checking for clues. All that was typed on it was *FAO R Richards* and *Urgent: to be read immediately upon receipt*. Intrigued, he opened it and began to read. After just one sentence he retreated to his inner sanctum; he didn't want anyone to see any unguarded reactions through the goldfish bowl glass walls of his outer office.

Ron

Don't return home tonight. We don't live there any more. The new owners are a lovely couple but I doubt very much that your presence would be welcome. The houses we've lived in have always been mine. This time I sold it and just didn't buy us another to live in together, since there is no more 'us'.

Where should you go? I don't really care. You are now in much the same position as when we met, with nothing but the clothes you are currently wearing. However, this time your choices are virtually unlimited due to the small fortune you must have accumulated, since none of your salary ever found its way to the joint bank account. I don't know how long you've been unfaithful to me, but I doubt you've squandered all of that money on mistresses. How many have you sent to that 'very good clinic'? You know, the 'very discreet' one you wanted to send me to?

I idolised you when we met. You were so charming, so handsome and strong, but more than that I admired your dedication to your studies, your determination to use education to escape the clutches of that dire council estate background. I was too naive back then to know you would also use people to get what you wanted, specifically me.

Yes, you used me to get access to my father's contacts and his financial backing; I learned that quite early on. You used me to deal with all the mundane trivia of life, leaving you to concentrate on your career. But I accepted the loss of my own career prospects, the loss of my friends and connection to my roots in our chase around the country for the next career move for you. As I've got older and less attractive to you (if I ever was), you've ignored me for the most part, or rather you don't even notice if I'm there or not. Sex (I won't dignify it by saying 'made love' as you've never been concerned about my pleasure, only your own) has been increasingly rare. I could bear all of that.

You knew there was only one thing I wanted in return for my selfless support of you, and you reneged on our deal. You crossed the boundary of my tolerance when you referred to my child as a thing to be disposed of. Now you must pay the price.

The easy part for you will be rebuilding the base fabric of your life, all the things that I always took care of for you. For the first time in your life you will have to buy a house and furnish it, clothe and feed yourself, deal with utility companies and household finances. Do you know how to cook? How to use a vacuum cleaner or washing machine? I realise you will not find it a problem financially, and that you will probably use that famous charm to inveigle some other woman into doing all this for you - in time - but at least I shall have the satisfaction of knowing that right now you will struggle. My own time, effort and money are now for my own benefit, mine and my child's.

How high you have flown, very much in the public eye. Do you worry about how vulnerable that makes you? How rabid other, younger, men are to bring you crashing back down? All they need is the right ammunition...

I have more than ammunition; I have a bomb that will blow your reputation sky high. I have irrefutable evidence of your activities that will sound the death knell on the only thing you care about. I took copies before you shredded them of every document you ever had in your study. You thought they were safely locked away, didn't you. But I'm a very thorough housekeeper and found the hiding place where you kept the key. And among those documents were your computer passwords. Yes, I have everything I need.

So, should you be worried?

Not if you leave me and my child alone. You made it abundantly clear that you don't want a child; I want to feel sure you won't act differently if the primal drive to pass on your genes should get the better of you. The evidence is safe in my keeping. It will only be released if you try to find me or interfere in my life, or my child's, or indeed if I should die in suspicious circumstances. You see, I don't trust you. I know how ruthless you can be and don't discount any action you might be tempted to pursue to get your own way. Leave us in peace and you will be safe.

No longer yours, sincerely or otherwise,
Daphne

~~~

She had prepared well, had a whole other identity set up with which to settle into life in Doumaine des Pins; she knew it to be a pretty little village on the Canal du Midi, having once visited there during her childhood travels with her French maternal grandmother. She had sworn to go back one day and now that day had come. Ron was totally unaware she had dual citizenship, French and British. He'd never been interested enough in her to find out about her family and now there were none left alive to question about her possible whereabouts. *Christ,* she thought, *he doesn't even know I speak French fluently. And with my legal change of name in France there is even less chance he will be able to follow the trail.*

There would be no difficulty completing the purchase of the small house on the edge of the village. Every day she would be able to look out onto the vineyards and fields of sunflowers. *I've always loved yellow, such a happy colour.* She would learn to appreciate food as the French did, learn more about her heritage, while her daughter flourished in the warmth of a culture in which children were important, the very centre and purpose of life. From an internet cafe she notified the agents of her expected date of arrival and then deleted the email account she'd used for contact with them. When she left she dumped the pay-as-you-go phone she'd been using in a large, smelly bin in a side alley.

Whilst laying her false trails, with their scattering of clues to her presence there, she had dressed, looked and behaved as Ron would remember her. Each day she had smoothed her hair up into a tidy knot and applied careful makeup to emphasise her large grey eyes and give her rather thin lips a better shape. Her clothes were elegant, their lines chosen to make the most of her puny stature.

Now I'm pregnant I might even get a cleavage for the first time in my life, she thought as she dressed in those clothes for the last time and felt a slight tenderness in her breasts.

For a week she had settled her hotel bills and paid for sundry other items with her credit card. With that, and use of her mobile phone, any investigator worth his salt, let alone with Ron's contacts, would easily follow her movements within the various cities, right up until her deliberate trail just stopped. It would probably take them a while, though, to figure out which city she might be in at any one time, and which city or nearby town she might have chosen to stay in long-term. They would have to check out a vast area of England before they could discount all of her apparent options.

Each time she had travelled she used the facilities in department stores to assume her disguise; she dressed as Ron's wife when she entered the stores, but left wearing charity shop clothes, devoid of makeup and with a white, permed wig. No one notices little old ladies; the eyes just skim over the surface, details aren't remembered. As she had been ignored for most of her life she had become a people-watcher; now she found it easy to reproduce an old woman's walk to match her disguise. She quietly shuffled along, clutching her large, dull shopping bag, and just faded into the background.

Her last journey in disguise took her from Manchester to Euston train station. As she had plenty of time before the departure of the Dover train she decided to walk along Euston Road to St Pancras International. It was a busy, rather ugly route, but she knew there would be the delight at the end of approaching one of the greatest Victorian buildings in London. Indeed, her eyes were so firmly fixed on the magnificent Gothic red brick facade that she very nearly blew her cover. In stepping back to better see the famous hotel clock tower she felt the thud of a taxi door into her back.

"Get out of the way!" a female voice exclaimed crossly.

Daphne stumbled forward, the breath driven from her body by the force of the car door slamming into her. As she looked over her shoulder, she was suddenly grateful she was winded and unable to speak, for her voice would have given her identity away. The woman was ignoring her, her full attention on the man at the rear of the taxi, who was taking a large suitcase out of the boot; that man was none other than Ron.

"For goodness' sake, Zara, do you really need so much for just a weekend?" he asked his companion. "This thing weighs a ton." He dumped the suitcase on the pavement unceremoniously and turned back for his own small bag.

While his attention was still diverted, Daphne resumed her bent posture and retreated at her old lady pace.

Zara sidled up to Ron and took his arm. "Darling, you know you like me to look good when we're out together," she said, "and anyway, there's loads of room in it to bring you back some nice new clothes from Paris. I know all the best places to re-equip you."

Daphne's sharp ears still heard their conversation, even over the traffic noise. She felt laughter bubbling inside, remembering why he needed 're-equipping'.

"I could do that here in London." Ron was hardly mollified and stomped off towards the Eurostar terminal with Zara struggling in her stilettos to keep up.

"Don't be such a grumpy-wump." Her voice was petulant but then changed, took on a more sultry tone as she caught up with him and squeezed his arm to her side. "It's so romantic along the Seine in the Spring; we can drink wine and really relax, forget all the nasty things she did to you."

So you want my castoff husband, do you? Better prepare for disappointment, Zara, I know that tone of voice; you won't be luring him off for dirty weekends for long.

Allons-y, Amélie; time for the last stage of our journey.

~~~

Marie-Anne put down her pen and looked around their room approvingly as she sealed the envelope. Her eyes followed a few motes of dust, dancing in the fingers of early morning sunlight that slipped through the partially drawn blinds. Their warmth caressed a gentle blush into her daughter's creamy, perfect skin and brought out the many-hued glory of Amélie's chestnut-bright hair where it fanned out over the pillow.

Even in her sleep she smiles.

When they returned to France, Amélie's wide circle of friends were always avid for details of the adventures she described so vividly in her many postcards to them. She was doing very well in school and special treats during their August travels were a reward for her hard work. Her first birthday had been spent in Scotland, the second in Ireland. As she got older they went further afield. Marie-Anne encouraged her to choose their destinations, agreeing if Amélie could tell her a little about the country she chose; for her tenth birthday she had asked to see New York.

What will the special treat be in this amazing city? Marie-Anne wondered.

Marie-Anne turned back to the little desk and addressed the envelope to Mr R Richards then popped it into her bag. A rustle of sheets behind her was quickly followed by a huge hug; Amelie always woke and was out of bed as if the spring had been released from a jack-in-the-box.

"Bonjour, Maman." Amélie rushed over to the window and pulled the cord to draw the blinds right back. "Oh, c'est incroyable!" She craned her neck to see all round.

Her daughter's voice was the music that filled Marie-Anne's days with love and laughter. "In English, Amélie," she said. "While we're in America we must speak English."

As this was not so much a second language as an equal language for Amélie it took no time at all for her to mentally shift gears. "Come and look, Maman, everything is so tiny down there, little toy cars and people!"

Marie-Anne went over to join Amélie, gazing down at the busy street nineteen storeys below. "Mon dieu, you are growing so fast, chérie," she said.

"In English, Maman," Amélie said, with a big cheeky grin, before dancing away into the bathroom with the grace of a young gazelle.

"Less of your lip, young lady," Marie-Anne called, "or

I might change my mind about buying you some American clothes. I might decide to only get you a new school uniform and shoes when we get home."

A bright head popped round the bathroom door, grey eyes wide and excited. Amélie pulled the toothbrush out of her mouth. "Can I choose them?"

"Choose the uniform?"

"Mummy!" Amélie's wail was drawn out several seconds.

Marie-Anne laughed. "Of course you can, *ma petite;* whatever you want on your special day."

"And can we go to the Statue of Liberty, right to the top? And get ice cream? And a burger? And go up in a helicopter?"

"All at the same time?" Marie-Anne took a tissue from the box and wiped toothpaste from Amélie's chin, then shadow-boxed her nose. "Come on, Amélie, hurry up and get ready or we won't get any of it done," she said, then went to gather what she would need for a day out.

Amélie didn't need a second invitation.

On the way out Marie-Anne popped the envelope into the post box in the hotel lobby. She stood there a moment, imagining Ron's feelings when he received it, knowing he would be expecting it after receiving nine others, one each year. Would he dread it dropping through the letter box? Would he hesitate before opening it? A secret little smile curved her lips as she imagined the scene.

"Come on, Maman! What are we waiting for?"

She took her daughter's hand and they went out into the sunshine and bustle of people and traffic that was New York.

Amélie, you will never know how much pleasure that annual envelope gives me.

For in the envelope was just one thing: a photo of her

daughter. And across it, in black capitals, were the words
THE DAUGHTER YOU WILL NEVER HAVE.

Decimal Point

Martha pushed the back door closed with one hip and gratefully let the four carrier bags slide to the floor. There were white ridges across the inside of her fingers from the weight of her shopping; she gingerly flexed them, then rubbed them against each other to bring some life back.

"Jack!" she called up the stairs. "Put your bike away in the garage, please, before it gets nicked."

There was a thundering down the stairs as she started to unpack. "Sorry, Little Woman," he said and ruffled her hair in passing. At six foot two he dwarfed his mother.

"Don't do that!" She slammed a bag onto the kitchen table and grabbed the first couple of cans to put away in the cupboard.

Jack looked sheepish and went out to move his bike from the drive, where he'd carelessly dumped it on his way in. When he returned he quietly started unpacking one of the bags. "Bad day?" he asked after a while. "Sit down and I'll make you a cuppa."

She slid into a chair and cradled her head in both hands, fingers laced through her short curly hair. "I don't know which I miss most," she said, "my car or my job."

"I guess that depends on whether it's a work day or a shopping day," Jack said. He picked up a bag of potatoes and checked the weight printed on it. "Or both. This is heavy stuff, Mum. You should have given me a list; I could have picked this stuff up after lectures."

"Hey, the only advantage of being a checkout chick is

the staff discount."

Jack frowned. "I hate you doing that job."

"It's paying some of the bills so don't knock it," she said and stretched her arms up, arching her back and rotating some of the kinks out of her neck. "I need to make that redundancy money last as long as possible."

"But someone with your qualifications and experience shouldn't be wasting away in a menial job." He added milk to the two mugs and passed one over.

Martha took it gratefully and blew on it to cool the first sip. "You know as well as I do that, in this area, my skills were only useful to *BioMed*."

"So we should move," he said.

"To Czechoslovakia? Mmmm..." She put on a mock thoughtful face, one finger to the side of her mouth. "The relocation offer was very generous, and I've heard the brand new facilities there are excellent."

He grinned. "Maybe not quite that far."

"We're not going anywhere, not so close to your finals," she said and got up to start preparing a bolognese. "Get your degree and then we'll have a rethink."

~~~

The next two months passed with both mother and son preoccupied. Martha had expected Jack to be spending a lot of time revising for his exams. She supposed that he had done so as he appeared nervous about the results coming out but quietly confident that he'd done the best he was capable of. Now, though, when he wasn't conferring with her over their latest job applications, or doing his part-time bar job, he spent every moment in his bedroom. There'd be sudden bursts of music, excited one-sided chatter (she assumed Skype or mobile to his friends) and long, long periods of silence. Normally it was a series of requests to turn his music down, so what was with the silence? And when they were together why did it feel like his mind was on another planet most of the time?

What really puzzled her, though, was why she hadn't yet had a letter requesting return of all that money. *Good grief,* she thought, *for that big an overpayment of redundancy money I'd expect panic phone calls, even a visit from the Finance Manager; something, surely?*

But day after day she worked in the supermarket, worrying about the bills that couldn't be pared down any more, while the money sat there in her account, waiting for the repayment instructions that never came. *Should I contact them?* she wondered for the zillionth time, only to tell herself again that she should let it ride as long as possible, gain her some interest while it was possible.

Her reverie was broken by a loud whooping from Jack's bedroom, quickly followed by a sound like lumber falling down the stairs. She looked up, bemused, as he rushed into the room.

"We've done it, Mum!" Jack said and lifted her into a bear hug, her feet dangling while he whirled her round the kitchen.

"Done what?" she finally managed to ask once she was back on the ground and able to breathe again.

"*Argot* has just run without a glitch for a solid week. We've finally debugged it!"

"What?"

He grabbed her handbag and keys and thrust them into her hands. "Come on, we're going to celebrate tonight." He pulled her towards the door. "We're meeting Harry and Dave down *The Crown* - we'll tell you all about it there."

It was obvious she'd get no sense from him until then so she pulled the light shawl she favoured for summer evenings off the back of a chair and allowed herself to be chivvied out the door.

~~~

The bar was busy but Harry and Dave were just grabbing a newly vacated table when they arrived. Jack pushed her towards them and signalled over that he'd get a round in.

"Hello, Harry, Dave," she nodded to each of them and sat down. "I haven't seen you for ages. How did the exams go?"

Dave wrinkled his nose. "OK, I suppose. They're over, anyway, so now we just wait and see."

"Mrs B," Harry said, kissing the back of her hand before sitting down, "I still salivate when I think about that beef stew and if I hear you're making another paella I'll be there before you can turn round."

Martha smiled at such enthusiasm. "You know you're both welcome, any time." She draped her shawl over the chair back then searched their faces for clues. "So, what's all the excitement about?"

Jack returned with a tray and four drinks so there was another delay while they all got settled. Martha found she was starting to get excited too, just from the vibes coming off the three close friends. They'd been inseparable since first meeting at the local university for their computing course. Harry and Dave were far from home and had appreciated the home comforts that Martha offered, whilst Jack had made full use of their student accommodation as crash pads, away from his mother. She understood his need for a private life and was happy with the situation, provided he let her know he wouldn't be home.

"Mum, you are looking at three geniuses," Jack said

with a huge grin, then a mock-puzzled face. "Geniuses? Genii? What's the correct plural of genius?"

"We are!" They chorused and clinked glasses before taking large swallows from their pint glasses.

"So what," Martha said, "is Argot?" Jack opened his mouth but his mother held up a hand, knowing him too well. "*Apart* from group slang," she said sternly.

"It is the most incredible game that will keep players hooked for *years*!" Harry said.

"And we developed it!" Dave chimed in, punching the air and displaying a gaping hole in the armpit of his *Lamb of God* tee.

"OK," she said. "Is it anything to do with slang?"

"Well, yes and no, Mrs B," Harry said. "There's the double strand - the adventure and quest side, Jason and the Argonauts kind of thing, but for those in the know there is the added power that comes from realising there's a secret argot, sort of a Masonic inner circle you can only enter if you learn it."

"Right, so what's the game all about?"

"Well, you know I've been a gamer ever since I could hold a joystick," Jack said, "and I've tried just about all of them at some time or another." He nodded to his friends. "Harry and Dave are much the same. We've played the shoot 'em ups, and city building, and racing, and world domination... You name it, we've tried it. Nothing was exactly what we wanted. Nothing held our attention for that long on its own. What we've done is create a game that can be played on many levels of interest for *years*, getting more and more complex the longer you're in it."

He stopped to take another drink and gather his thoughts. Martha sat quietly, giving him time.

"The basics of it, at the start, are that you can define up to five avatars, and as there are five planets you can have one on each, or concentrate on building your power base on just one planet, or any combination you choose at any time. You can have a worker to earn *Peta*, currency, to pay for another's actions, you can thieve, you can manipulate outcomes as a politician or leader of military forces, or spy, or form a guerrilla terror group - whatever you can imagine you can do."

"Yeah," Harry added, "and the sneakier, more selfish, more power-hungry and corrupt you are-"

"Like you in real life then," Dave said. A brief grapple nearly had them off their chairs. "Aw, stop it man!" Dave said, between laughter and a groan.

"- the better you'll succeed," Harry continued, with Dave's head in an armlock. "The whole point is to be the puppet master of as many other players as you can. You can't just choose to be at the top of any heap, though: you have to earn your right to get to that position of power."

"The really addictive bit, though," Jack told her, "is it's a network game so you have to get inside the heads of the other regular gamers, get to know who you can form alliances with, who will stab you in the back the first chance they get. And you can interface with the real world, exchanging real life items, even cash, for *Peta* another player has earned."

Harry interrupted. "This is going to make us millionaires, Mrs B! We'll be able to retire at thirty and live a life of luxury if we want."

"Or run a really cool company for games developers," Dave added, his eyes sparkling.

"Or be so addicted to your own game you never come up for air," Martha said drily. She surveyed the eager faces round the table. "I'm not a gamer -"

"That'd be the day," Jack said.

"- so I can't comment on the idea or the impact it might

106

- or might not - have on the gaming world. I think you might find, though, that you've just completed the easy part."

"Easy part?" Jack's wasn't the only incredulous reaction. "We've devoted over two years of hard slog writing this software! We've missed countless parties and hours of sleep developing it."

"I have no doubt of that, just as I didn't doubt I'd done the hard part when I finished my first novel and published it."

Harry and Dave looked at each other. "We didn't know you're a novelist," Dave said.

"It's a hobby," Martha said with a shrug of her shoulders. "My point is that, as a self-published author, I then investigated the next stage, specifically the marketing and promotion. For myself I decided that was all a terrible bore and I wouldn't waste my precious free time doing something that didn't interest me. You won't have that option if you want to become millionaires from it. Now you might be lucky and have it go viral, but that relies on an initial push in the right direction from the right people. How well do you know your demographic? Is that likely to happen?"

"We have a big enough social network between us to start things off. Word will spread pretty fast on Facebook, Twitter, YouTube," Jack said. "Globally we're looking at tens of millions."

"Globally," she repeated. "So how many languages are you going to release it for?" Martha asked. "If it's not just for the UK, Australasia and America you'll need a professional translation service; do you intend to concentrate first on China, Japan, Korea, Malaysia? Or EU countries?" She could see reality starting to kick in and took pity on them. "Look, I don't want to piss on your firework tonight. You've done well to get this far and deserve to celebrate your achievement, but just take away a few thoughts from it to ponder over tomorrow."

They nodded solemnly.

"I suggest you write this down as you may not remember - or even believe it - by tomorrow." She gave each of them a pen and a page out of the notebook she always carried in her handbag.

"1) See a solicitor to set up a company officially and sort out how to go about internationally copyrighting your game.

"2) Define how many gamers will be in the user testing group and how you will recruit them, remembering to factor into the testing all the various devices players will want to run it on.

"3) Decide on translation issues."

"Slow down, Mum," Jack complained, glancing round to see if he was the only one struggling to keep up.

She gave them a few minutes then continued, pausing when necessary.

"4) Pay for registration of a company domain name.

"5) Find a really good web designer as you'll need something that looks exciting and provides fast and secure payments and downloads.

"6) Consult with an expert on piracy prevention.

"7) Define a timeline: you'll want to start building the buzz a month before release date, and ideally you want to be in position for the Christmas sales market. Are you going to rely on social networking or is there a possibility of getting a mention on TV shows like that BBC one - what is it? *Click?* And maybe radio interviews, magazine articles, that kind of thing.

"8) Decide if it will be purely online sales from your web site or if it will need producing and distributing to physical stores and/or online stores like Amazon.

"9) Find out what company start-up assistance is being offered by the government, central and local.

"10..." She paused and stood up, straightened her blouse then picked up the tray. "I'll get us all another drink in before I tell you number ten." She went to the bar, wondering if she was about to really drop herself in it with her number ten.

When she returned they were looking very doleful.

"You weren't wrong when you said we'd done the easy bit," Harry said mournfully. "How do you know all that stuff?"

"A combination of work and my writing," she said. "Just because I don't do it doesn't mean I don't know about it."

"We're dead in the water," Dave said. "There's no way we can fund all that." He pushed his piece of paper away from him and his shoulders slumped.

"So much for celebrating," Jack agreed.

Martha sat back down and distributed the drinks. "You haven't heard number ten yet," she reminded them and waited until she had their full attention. "If Jack reckons the game is that good, if he's got that much faith in it, then I've got enough faith in him to back the three of you. I'll finance you to the tune of £100,000 for a 10% share of the company," she said.

Jack's jaw just dropped. "But, Mum... We're piss poor, have been since you lost your job. Where will you find dosh like that?"

Martha blushed. "I'm finding that I might do quite well in some aspects of your game," she admitted. "I, er, didn't tell *BioMed* they'd made a mistake when they paid me my redundancy money. With the time I'd been there and the salary I was on when I left, it should have been twelve thousand, eight hundred and fourteen pounds and fifty six pence paid into my account. Someone at some stage put the decimal point in the wrong place, though, and my account was credited with one hundred and twenty eight thousand, one hundred and forty five pounds sixty."

As realisation dawned a big grin replaced Jack's look of hopeless defeat. "You sly old thing, you," he said.

"Less of the 'old' if you don't mind," she said and slapped his arm.

"Hear that, lads? My ever so honest mother has kept shtum about money she's not entitled to. Would that count as theft in a court of law, do you reckon?"

Martha's blush deepened. "It's not like I spent it," she protested. "I know I lost my loyalty to the company when they decided the cheap option was more important than the people who were making them all that money, but I don't intend stealing it. I was just earning some interest while waiting to hear from them, but I guess it's not been noticed, what with all the upheaval of moving to Czechoslovakia." She took a big sip of her wine. "I guess it won't come to light until the accounts go to the auditors next April, so..." she took another gulp of wine, "umm... until then I'm willing to risk using it."

Jack looked sober again. "And if I'm wrong? What will you do next April if I lose that money?"

She took both his hands in hers. "Jack, I trust your judgement. If you tell me this is one of those chances in life you should grab with both hands, then I believe you and the next thing we do will be to toast the new company."

Jack straightened in his chair. Martha felt great pride in her son and could almost see the mantle of manhood settling round his shoulders. He raised his glass.

"To *embee games*," he said solemnly, the question in his eyes.

Harry and Dave looked at each other and nodded, "Good name," Dave said.

They all held their glasses together a moment, then Jack whooped loud and long, turning all heads in their direction.

"Let the party begin!"

~~~

The boys worked flat out to get everything set up officially. Martha felt very proud of them: the professional attitude they were taking to their venture, how smart, how adult, Jack looked in a suit, and how well he maintained his cool when things didn't go quite as smoothly as they'd like. His most regular gripe was the continental drift pace of the officials they dealt with - except when they wanted paying. He was, however, developing an impressive ability to deal with them, polite but assertive. They were coming to know that, young as he was, he wouldn't accept excuses that weren't backed with good reasons, wouldn't readily accept no for an answer.

She was also extremely worried; she hadn't told them the first repayment demand had arrived in the post a few hours before she transferred the money to the *embee games* bank account. She'd shredded that one; she hadn't signed for it so could legitimately claim it had been lost in the post. A fortnight later an email arrived; she deleted the account and set up a new one, telling Jack that she'd had 'a problem' with the old one.

"Mum, you're in business with three IT experts." Jack shook his head, baffled. "It would be a poor shout if we couldn't sort it out for you," he said.

"Oh, I didn't want to bother you; you've more important things to think about right now. Besides, it was easy enough to start a new account." Which was true, setting it up was quick and easy; the difficult, time consuming part was sorting out all the sites she had linked to the old email and letting all her contacts know about the change.

Two months into their venture, having nervously watched hundreds, then thousands, paid out of the account, Martha got home from work to find Jack waiting for her, an official looking envelope in his hand. She did her best to act normally but felt the blood drain from her face.

"What a day," she said. "You would not believe how stupid some people can be when they're shopping. And the staff aren't much better." She sat down before her legs gave out on her.

Jack tapped the envelope against his opposite thumb, looking serious. "Mum, are we in trouble over that money?"

"What do you mean?"

"This looks very official - I had to sign for it, and it's from a big firm of accountants in London." Jack held up his hand as Martha started to speak. "And don't lie to me, Mum. I know you're dealing with *embee* finances, but I also know we're not at the stage of needing accountants of this stature. The only valid option I can think of is that it's about that redundancy money."

"I can't know what's in a sealed envelope, can I?" She accepted the envelope with feigned indifference.

"You haven't answered my question. Are *BioMed* accountants demanding repayment?"

She stood slowly, drawing herself up to her full five foot four inches, and raised her chin defiantly. "I trust you to deal with the game and the business. Trust me to deal with the finances," she said. "I'm going up to get changed. Tea's in half an hour."

"Mum, we've got to talk about this!" he called after her.

"Don't worry," she said from half way up the stairs, "If it comes to it I'll see about remortgaging the house." There was no way she was going to admit she'd already asked, and been turned down.

With each communication over the next few months Martha knew the accountants' patience was wearing thinner. Each time she delayed responding until the last possible day to eke out the time she had before they acted. She wasn't at all clear what her legal position would be if *embee* didn't manage projected sales by the end of the year, as by her reckoning that would be the longest she could stall them.

~~~

It was Christmas Eve and sales had been ramping up exponentially during the previous two weeks. They'd had to install a second server to cope with the demand. Jack was carefully watching activity on them, praying there wouldn't be a last-minute crash, while Harry and Dave tried to keep up with the Facebook and Twitter activity. Martha had kept her finger on the company's financial pulse. She was sure she'd lost about a stone with the stress of it all.

"We might just do it," she said, with one eye on the clock.

The numbers crept upwards as the second hand swept its circles on the wall.

"Here we go," she said nervously, "just one more needed."

The boys all looked at the clock and started the countdown. "Ten, nine, eight..."

"Come on," Martha wailed to her computer screen.

"... seven, six, five..."

113

"Here," she said excitedly, "I think it will... Yes! Our first million!"

The four of them danced around the room and hugged and kissed and cried.

"Happy Christmas, Mum," Jack said, holding her above the floor in a hug. He put her back on the ground, took a step back and held her hands. "Thank you." He ruffled her hair, then sat at the computer and logged into *embee games'* bank account. He grinned over his shoulder. "Now then, Little Woman, shall we authorise that repayment?"

More books by Jay Howard

Novels:
Changes:
Book 1 Never Too Late
Book 2 New Beginnings

Short stories:
As the Sun Goes Down

About Jay Howard

Jay currently lives in Somerset, which she considers to be a gem among English counties. She has lived and worked in many places in England, Wales, Alberta and British Columbia. Holding dual citizenship through her father, who was born in Toronto, a visit to her 'other country' included a stay in her father's city followed by the four day train journey to the West coast. She describes the trip as 'the only way for an English visitor to start to comprehend the vastness and diversity of this land'.

Whilst admitting that trying so many different areas of work may not be ideal for most people, Jay believes that her experiences have given her insights that enrich her writing. She describes writing as 'enormously enjoyable and satisfying, but second only to golf in the level of frustration that must be endured to achieve the desired goal'.

31237410R00067

Made in the USA
Charleston, SC
10 July 2014